I0781112

A CHRISTMAS *Family*

A Novella

—SMALL TOWN CHRISTMAS—
BOOK 9

❋ ❋ ❋

D. ALLEN

DN Publishing

A Christmas Family
Small Town Christmas, Book 9
Copyright © 2024 by D. Allen
Batavia, NY

www.DavidNethBooks.com

ISBN: 978-1-963602-09-8
First Edition

Subscribe to the author's newsletter for updates and exclusive content:
DavidNethBooks.com/Newsletter

Follow the author at:
www.facebook.com/DavidNethBooks
www.instagram.com/dnpublishing

Also by D. Allen

<u>Montana Beach</u>
Summer Stay

Summer Job

Summer Nights

<u>Small Town Christmas</u>
A Christmas Reunion

A Christmas Charade

A Christmas Spark

A Christmas Song

A Christmas Departure

A Christmas Wedding

A Christmas Escape

A Christmas Renovation

A Christmas Family

<u>Standalones</u>
Snow After Christmas

Thanksgiving Day Parade

December 21st
Collette

❅ ❅ ❅

I'm out the door by seven o'clock in the morning, just as I had done before I retired. Most retirees talk about having time to adjust to their new lives without the obligation of going to work. I've never had such luxury. I went right from teaching to volunteering at various organizations that I hold near and dear to my heart. I love it so much that I wish we didn't live in a world where we had to work. Perhaps people would be nicer if they found things to do to help other people as a reason to get out of bed in the morning. Then again, a lot of people rely on the structure that a regular day job provides.

My car slides into the parking lot of St. Mary's not even ten minutes later, and only five minutes after that

I'm in the warm embrace of the church's basement community hall. There are tables lined along one wall with baked goods placed in disarray.

I set my cinnamon muffins down on a free spot on the table toward the end of the long display, admiring the red and green wicker basket that I placed them in. I've always admired that basket but it's better to give than to…well, *hoard*.

What's the use of having stuff if you can't enjoy it or share it with others?

Maureen Powell comes out of the kitchen just as I'm slipping off my coat.

"Oh good! You're here!" she says with a bright smile. "I was hoping you'd get in early like me."

"We're both a little nuts, Mo," I say. "It's not even seven-thirty and the sale doesn't start for another several hours. It's not going to take us that long to set up."

"No, but I'm sure Nancy will bring in breakfast for all of the volunteers, and I want to mark down who brought what, so we can return any dishes that came in that aren't meant to go out, and then we can write thank-you notes afterwards."

I nod. Nancy Slater is known for making a bigger production out of things than is necessary. Then again, when her daughter is rolling in the dough, it's nice to flaunt it on your friends every once in a while.

"Are you going to stay through to the sale?" Maureen asks.

I shake my head. "No, but I wish I could. I have some Christmas shopping to finish up, and wrapping. And I'm volunteering at the library tonight, so I guess there'll probably be a nap in there somewhere too."

Maureen clutches her chest and laughs. "Oh yes! I'm sure tonight will be an early bedtime for me too, since I'll miss my regular afternoon nap."

"Well, you have me for a little bit." I put my hands on my hips and look around. "Most of the stores don't open until nine, so I'm yours until then. What can I help with?"

Maureen puts me to work laying out tablecloths on the round tables scattered around the space. I help unload the folding chairs from the cart in the corner and place six at each table.

When Maria Barlow arrives, she brings with her several homemade centerpieces to lay on each of the tables. Even with the cheap green plastic tablecloths and the red paper doilies, adding some berries and green leaves with a bow tied around them helps cheer the place up.

"Can we get some Christmas music going?" I ask Maureen. "Something playing quietly in the background. Nothing too loud. Maybe even something instrumental?"

Any effort to make it seem like more than a church basement would bring additional cheer to this sale. There's a Christmas tree near the stairs, but it's shorter than me—which is saying something—and only the few pre-lit lights are on and a few scant ornaments. We need a little something more to bring in the excitement of the season. Judging by the baked goods on the table, a lot of these treats will be shared with loved ones on Christmas in only a couple days.

"I'm on it!" Maureen calls before disappearing back into the kitchen.

As assumed, Nancy brings a whole breakfast feast for the few volunteers when she arrives. Scrambled eggs, biscuits, fruit, orange juice, chocolate milk, and even her own specialty brand of coffee. And it isn't a Nancy Slater-sanctioned meal without her own paper plates and plastic silverware.

"Nancy, this looks delicious," Maria says as she helps Nancy unload the containers of food.

"Oh, this was nothing." Nancy waves it off and passes out paper plates. "You know I love doing this sort of thing."

As the volunteers sit to eat, they each share their holiday plans. Maureen and her husband plan on spending Christmas Day with their son, Isaac, and his wife, Tori. Nancy is having both of her daughters over and their husbands, and all the grandkids. Maria is doing the same, although her older daughter, Olivia, has already come in from Columbus, Ohio, with her family and so the house is, as she puts it, a "war zone."

"What are you planning on doing, Collie?" Maria asks once everyone else has had a chance to share.

I shrug, being the only one in the group without children or grandchildren. And although Nancy had lost her husband years ago and was *technically* single again, I am the only one who never married.

"Nothing too fancy. Just having a Hallmark movie marathon, treating myself to a nice big meal, and then probably settling in with a good book under the Christmas lights." I smile. It's not much, but it's mine. My alone time is something I've grown comfortable with over the years.

The girls all make sympathetic noises.

"Aw, honey!" Nancy rubs my leg.

"You can come with me to my son's house if you'd rather have company," Maureen offers. "I know he wouldn't mind, and we'll have plenty of food."

I shake my head and raise my hand in objection. "No, that's okay. I'll be fine. Really. You should all have the private time with your families. I'll see you girls after the holiday. It's only one day. I can survive."

Maria makes a face. "Aw, but it's Christmas."

I nod. "I know. And I'll be okay. I'm a big girl."

"And you'll get even bigger if we keep eating these biscuits," Maureen jokes. She winks at me, sensing that I need a change in conversation.

"Everything was delicious, Nancy," I say. "Thanks for bringing it."

"Of course! Thanks for helping!" She stands and begins collecting everyone's plates. "Let's clean up so we can get this place spick and span."

"Do you mind if I take some of these leftovers up to Father Thomas?" Maria asks.

"Go ahead! Lord knows I don't need them in my house. I'll have enough junk food in the next couple days. No sense in adding anymore."

I stand and help with the rest of the cleanup. It doesn't take long, since there are so many of us helping. We move on to finish setting up for the bake sale. I help Maureen make signs with the names of the breads, pies, muffins, and other baked goods. Nancy and Maria make sure everything is ready to make sales: cash, carrying bags, and even some plastic cutlery in case anyone wanted to stay and enjoy their treat in the hall.

By the time we're done, it's nearly ten o'clock.

"Oh, my! I need to get going." I reach for my coat and pull it on.

"Thank you for helping," Nancy says.

"Not a problem." After my coat is on, each of the girls give me a hug. When it's Maureen's turn, she whispers, "Are you sure you don't want to come over for Christmas dinner?"

"Yes, I'm sure. But thank you for the offer. I do appreciate it."

She gives me a smile, then says, "See you at Christmas Eve mass?"

"Before that, probably. Won't you need help taking everything down tomorrow?"

"I would love that, thank you!" Nancy chirps from across the room.

Maureen smiles at me. "Guess you're on the hook for tomorrow."

"And you too, Mo!" Nancy calls to her.

"Leave!" Maureen urges. "Save yourself before you're volunteered for anything else!"

I laugh and give a final wave to the girls before heading back out into the cold.

I'm very well aware that it's December 21st, and the bulk of my holiday shopping is done, thank you very much, but there are only a few last-minute things I need to grab before I see everyone one last time before Christmas.

My first stop is to the candy store on West Main Street. They make their own chocolate that is always the best last-minute Christmas gift for everyone. It's only adding to the sugar consumption that is inevitable, but it's the holidays. We all need to indulge every now and then.

My next stop is to the florist further down West Main Street. Beverly always helps me pick out the perfect floral arrangements for all of my friends. Every year I have them delivered on Christmas Eve, so their homes will look, feel, and smell wonderful for the season.

I make sure to add deliveries to my neighbors,

who have all been especially helpful already this winter season with the snow. I can handle a shovel pretty well, but it's nice to have some extra help in the cold.

I make a stop for coffee across town, then venture back to my house on Union Street. It's small, compact, and perfect for an old woman like me. I've had it about as long as I've been on my own, having only lived in an apartment on Bank Street for a year when I first moved out of my parents' house at nineteen years old.

After making myself a cup of tea, I flick on the electric fireplace that's replaced my wood-burning one, and settle on the couch. The Christmas tree sits in the corner and, even though the lights are off, the sunlight coming through the window catches the silver garland draped around the tree and sends beautiful sparkly reflections up on the ceiling and the surrounding walls.

This is my happy place. Something I think of all year long when I'm having a bad day. And to have this moment to be still and enjoy the latest Debbie Macomber Christmas book is something I wouldn't trade for anything in the world.

My happy place is apparently also very comfortable because before I know it, it's nearly three o'clock in the afternoon.

I don't go looking for naps. They just kind of find me.

Taking a quick sip of my tea, I'm not surprised to find that it's gone cold. I get up and make myself a fresh cup of coffee, which I pour into an insulated travel mug, and bundle myself up to head back out into the cold.

Since I first sat down, the weather has shifted and it isn't until I step outside that I see that it's snowing. And apparently has been snowing for some time.

My car is covered and I use my glove to brush away the snow from the doorframe so only a minimal amount falls inside when I open the door.

"Hi Miss Hopkins!" Kyle calls from next door. He's standing on the sidewalk in front of his house, propped against his shovel. I swear I see him out here nearly constantly throughout the winter. He must love the cold.

"Hi there!" I call back. "Sure is cold."

He nods. "Yeah. Do you want some help brushing off your car?"

I shake my head. "No, I'm okay. Thank you for offering, though!" I duck inside my car, pull out my snow brush from the back seat, and brush off the snow from all the windows. Luckily, it's all light and fluffy snow, so it falls off without having to scrape anything off.

Within minutes, I'm backing down the driveway, hearing the crunch of the snow beneath my tires. I wave to Kyle, who has cleared his walkways down to the pavement and is turning toward my sidewalk as I pull away.

I'll have to thank him later, I tell myself. *Maybe I can make him cookies. I'll have to stop at the store tomorrow morning to pick up more chocolate chips and flour.*

The drive to the library is slower than usual, but otherwise uneventful. Which is always a good thing when traveling in the winter time where so many things could go wrong.

"I'm so sorry I'm late," I tell Elaine, the librarian working the circulation desk. I unwrap my scarf from around my neck and peel off my coat, hanging it on a hook in the office behind the desk.

Elaine shoots me a look with a smirk. "Collette, you're a volunteer. You can do whatever you want."

"I know, but I don't want to leave you guys hanging." I come out from the office and take a look at the few piles of books on the desk. "Is there anything in particular you need done?"

"Nothing special. It's been a slow night with the snow and all."

"I'll get started on shelving these books then." I wheel the cart out from behind the desk and start in the non-fiction section.

Shelving books is easy work. It's stimulating enough that it keeps me busy, but not so mentally-consuming that I can't listen to an audiobook while putting the books away.

I spend the next half hour working my way

through the non-fiction section, but before I can move on to the fiction, I notice that the coffee station I had set up needs to be cleaned up. Upon closer inspection, I see that the coffee filter needs to be changed as well.

I spend some time getting that cleaned up before returning to shelving the books. After a few minutes in the fiction section, I notice a woman browsing a shelf of mysteries. She pulls a book, reads the back, then puts it back on the shelf, letting out a sigh.

"If you're looking for a good mystery, I like Tess Gerritsen," I tell her. "Or if you want something a little lighter, Sue Grafton is good too. And then there's always Janet Evanovich."

The woman smiles. "Tess Gerritsen isn't too gory?"

I shake my head back and forth. "She doesn't shy away from the realities of everything, but she's not gory for the sake of gore."

The woman glances back at the shelf. "But which one to start with?"

"If you're looking for a series, this is the start of a great one." I reach over and pull a copy of *The Surgeon* for her. "Or she has plenty of standalone titles as well."

The woman smiles and waves the book in the air. "I'll try this one. Thanks for the suggestion!"

I watch as the woman goes off to the checkout counter, then return to my cart full of books.

I spend the rest of my volunteer hours putting away all of the books on the cart. The process slows when I stop to clean up pencil marks from a few tables, refill the printers, and help Elaine decide on some new book display ideas.

When my shift is done, I wrap myself back up in my outerwear, bid Elaine and the other librarians goodnight, and head back out into the cold.

It's snowed again, so I spend some time brushing off my car, then proceed carefully onto Main Street. In the darkness, I admire the Christmas lights lining the street and the ones decorating the houses when I pull onto Union Street.

My house stands beautifully among the rest. The lights that I worked so hard to put up twinkle brightly under the freshly fallen snow, helping to bring holiday cheer to the whole street.

And yet, there's something that doesn't quite feel *right*. My day was full—my *life* has been full—but something is still missing.

I have a feeling I know what that something is, and it's something I'll never have.

DECEMBER 21ST

❄ ❄ ❄

One of the problems with getting old is that even though you have the time to sleep in, your body simply doesn't allow it. Ever since I got up to pee at four o'clock—my second trip to the bathroom last night—I've been tossing and turning in bed, completely restless and unable to fall back to sleep.

Finally, I roll over and glance at the clock. It's just after five o'clock. I suppose that's late enough to get up and start the day.

Shuffling into the kitchen, I pour myself a bowl of cereal—Cheerios and milk, the doctor says that any other cereal is too much sugar and that I should consider making eggs in the morning instead. Again, even though I have the time to make breakfast and wash the dishes, who wants to spend their time doing that? So I just eat my cereal in the kitchen, reading last week's *Pennysaver* yet again.

When I'm done, I visit the bathroom, brush my teeth, then bundle myself up to head out into the cold. I'm halfway through brushing off my car when I hear Clarice Henderson's voice call out from next door.

"Do you want me to send my boys over to help?"

I turn back to her and force a smile. This woman means well, but all of her offers for help make me feel like an invalid. "No, let them sleep in. I'll be okay!" I turn back and take one swipe of snow off the car when I hear her voice again.

"Are you sure?"

I give her a thumbs-up through my knitted gloves. Can't she take a hint? "Yes, thank you!"

She finally disappears back into the house, and I finish clearing the snow from my car.

Ten minutes later, I'm pulling into the gym parking lot and braving the cold as I power-walk inside.

"Merry Christmas," I say to the girl at the counter when I scan my membership card.

"Good morning, Mr. Marshall," she says. "You're here early."

"Couldn't sleep." I head off to the locker room and change into my gym clothes.

I like to start the day with a two-mile walk to get

the heart racing and the blood pumping. The doctor said it'll help prevent blood clots, which is one of the few things in this world that I'm afraid of. My brother died a few years ago when a blood clot in his leg made its way to his heart. By the time they discovered the clot, it was too late.

I get settled on a treadmill and watch CNN on one TV while keeping my eye on the local news on another.

"Hey, Eddie, how are ya?" Gary comes up on the treadmill beside me.

"Not bad. My elbow is starting to act up." I raise it and move my arm back and forth to work the elbow.

"Does that mean we're in for a storm?" Harry jokes when he comes up on the treadmill on my other side.

"Hey, if the system works, it works," I joke back.

"Do you think the Bills will win tomorrow?" Gary motions up at the local news TV.

"They've been doing good so far," Harry adds.

"Remember when we used to go out to the games?" I ask.

"No," Gary laughs. "I don't, actually!"

"That's because you never made it in from the parking lot!" Harry shoots back.

"Too drunk from tailgating," I add with a smile. Those were some fun times. About the only fun times I had had in my life. How our lives have changed.

That was before Gary and Harry had families. Lately they've been talking about their kids planning their weddings. Gary's daughter is pregnant, while Harry's son has three kids of his own.

"You guys going to go see your kids for the holidays?" I ask.

"Grant, Marcy, and the kids are coming over and we're going to Face-Zoom or Face Call or whatever video call thing that they call it nowadays," Harry says. "We're going to call Dillon out in Colorado. That way we can all see each other and he doesn't have to pay for airfare."

"It's a beautiful thing, technology, isn't it?" Gary asks.

Harry shrugs. "Sometimes, but I'd rather him home. It's better than not seeing him at all, though."

"That's true," I say.

"What about you?" Harry asks. "Are you going over to your neighbor's house?"

"Me?" I ask, looking between them.

"Why the hell would *I* go to my neighbor's house for Christmas?" Gary asks.

He means it as a joke, but it still stings. Just like Harry, Gary is happily married. Even if he and his wife don't have their kids at home with them for Christmas like they used to, they're still having Christmas together. This year they're probably going to their daughter's house.

As for me, I used to spend the holidays with my

brother and his wife. But since he passed away, his wife has moved down to Florida. We talk on the phone every once in a while, but it's become obvious that Doris and I only had any kind of relationship because of Dalton.

Last year the Hendersons invited me over since it was the first Christmas without having any family in the area, but I felt like I was intruding on their close family time. It just didn't quite feel right to me. Then again, I don't know if anything ever will.

"Um, I haven't really discussed it with the neighbors, but I might." I shrug. "I might just stay in and lay low too. It's not a big deal."

"No, you can't just stay home alone," Harry says. "Come on over if you don't have other plans. Janet always makes way too much food, so there will be more than enough for you."

Thankfully, the treadmill hits the two mile mark and I hit STOP. "Thanks for the offer. I'll think about it."

By the look on his face, we both know that I won't give it another thought, but we're polite enough not to mention it.

"I'll see you boys later. Have a good day!"

I head off to the locker room, where I strip, grab my shower caddy and towel, and take a shower.

After my shower, I wrap the towel around my waist as Gary comes back in, sweaty from his trek on the treadmill.

"Hey, it's okay to spend the holidays with other people," Gary says. "You don't have to turn us down. You're not imposing."

I nod and reach for my clothes from my locker. "Thank you for that, but I'll be fine. Really."

Gary studies me for a moment, then puts up his hands and smiles. "Suit yourself!" He heads off to his own locker.

I dress and bundle up for the cold weather. Outside, the sun has risen but, luckily, there hasn't been anymore snow. Which means that I can get in my car pretty quickly and head back home.

That's where I see the Henderson boys, Ryan and Blake, shoveling their driveway. I give them a wave as I pull onto the street, which has already been cleared by the snowplow.

"Morning, boys!" I call to them as I walk in the tires tracks I left in the driveway on my way out that morning.

"Morning, Mr. Marshall!" they call back.

I head inside, where I don a heavier jacket, a hat and gloves, then venture out into the garage to fire up the snowblower.

As the garage door lifts, I see that Ryan and Blake are working away at the snow on the sidewalk in front of my house with their shovels.

It's a nice gesture, but I hate it. I wish the Hendersons would stop seeing me as incapable and start seeing me more as an equal. I'm sixty-seven,

I'm not dead yet.

I start up the snowblower with the pull cord, shift it into gear, and take the first swipe down the side of the driveway, tossing the snow into the strip of grass between my driveway and the Henderson's. At the end of the driveway, I hold the brake and call to the boys.

"Thanks for helping, boys, but I can take it from here!"

Over the motor, Ryan—the older one—shouts back, "No, we can do it."

I push down the surge of annoyance that threatens to bubble over. "How about you boys do the sidewalk and the front porch and I'll take care of the driveway? I wouldn't feel right sitting inside while you're doing my work."

Blake nods. "I'm good with that."

Without waiting for another objection, I turn the blower around and start back up the driveway, cranking the blower to fire in the opposite direction.

It takes us twenty-five minutes to finish moving the snow. By the time I pull the snowblower back in the garage, the boys are finishing up on the front porch.

They come join me in the driveway after they're done.

Ryan nods to the car in the garage. "You got the Mustang covered up for the winter?"

I follow his gaze to my 1975 Mustang that takes

up most of my one-car garage. "Have to. Don't want any salt or snow getting on it. I wish I could store it in a place that I don't have to keep opening up, but it's survived this long, so I guess there's no harm in it."

"Every year, we know winter is officially over when we see you pulling it out and taking it for a drive," Blake adds.

"It'll be a while before that happens." I laugh. "It's my pride and joy. I have to take care of it. Hey, if you boys are interested, I could fire up the heater in the garage and you could help me tinker with it. There's a few things I was going to do in the spring, but I don't see why we can't do it now."

"We actually have a basketball game to get to in, like—" Ryan checks his phone. "—oh shoot, in an hour. We have to get going."

"Oh, but Mom wants us to invite you to dinner tonight," Blake says.

I wave it off, averting my eyes to the cleared driveway, studying the tire marks in the remaining snow from the snowblower. "I appreciate the offer, boys, but I'm an old man. I'll probably end up falling asleep at your house after the delicious feast your mother is sure to cook."

The boys shrug. "Okay. Well, if you change your mind, just come on over," Ryan says.

They start toward their house and I feel my heart sink a little. As much as I hate them insisting on helping, I do enjoy the company. But they're teenagers. They're busy. They don't want to stick around with an old man all day. And coming over for dinner would feel like an imposition. I already take them up on their offers too much.

"Good luck at your game," I say as they walk off. "And thanks for the help."

"Anytime," Blake says. "Just text us—or call us. We'll pick up for you."

I shake my head and watch as they disappear into the house. Then I go into the garage, let the door down, and head inside.

After stripping off my winter clothes, I settle on the couch and reach for the TV remote. I find some terrible Christmas special and, within minutes, feel my eyes begin to grow heavy as I start to drift off.

The doorbell wakes me up. I blink my eyes and look around, suddenly startled awake. The program I had been watching is over, and the station has moved on to a different terrible Christmas special.

Another ring of the doorbell tells me that I didn't imagine the first ring. Gripping the arm of the couch and the cushion beside me, I vault myself up onto my feet.

The doorbell rings a third time when I'm just about to the door and I swing it open violently. My anger quickly defuses when I see Clarice Henderson standing in the doorway.

"I'm sorry, did I wake you?" she asks.

If you hadn't intended to wake me, why did you ring the bell three times? I wonder, but keep it to myself.

"It's all right. Probably shouldn't sleep too long anyway, otherwise I won't be able to sleep tonight." I wave her in. "Come inside. Let me close the door and keep the heat in."

She steps inside, careful to keep her wet boots on the stone section of the entryway. "I don't mean to be a bother, it's just that the boys told me that you don't want to come for dinner. I'm afraid I must insist."

I start shaking my head before she's even finished speaking. "Clarice, I appreciate the offer, but—"

"But you've turned us down the last *three* times we've offered."

Maybe that was the reason for the three doorbell rings, I wonder.

"And each time you claimed to have plans and I've seen you through the window eating alone." Clarice shakes her head. "It's Christmas, and I'm putting my foot down about this." She crosses her arms for good measure.

There's no way I'm getting out of this without being a complete ass, and Ryan and Blake *did* just help me this morning with the snow in my driveway.

With a heavy sigh, I say, "Okay. I can come for dinner."

Clarice beams. "Oh good! Yay! Feel free to come over anytime, but we should be eating around five o'clock."

I glance at the watch on my wrist. That's only two hours away. I nod. "Okay. Thanks for the invite."

"Anytime! I mean it, *anytime*. You're always welcome."

I open the door as a silent cue to have her leave. If I'll be spending the evening intruding on her family, I need the next two hours to be by myself. "I'll see you in a little bit."

❄ ❄ ❄

"WHO WANTS DESSERT?" Clarice asks as her husband, Martin, gets up and begins clearing the table of the dirty plates.

"Dessert?" I blurt. "After that big meal?"

Clarice had prepared a full roast chicken with stuffing, mashed potatoes, gravy, cranberry sauce, green beans, and corn. Not to mention the homemade bread and salad that came prior to the meal.

"This is Mom's pre-Christmas test run," Ryan explains.

"You cook the same large meal twice in one week?" I ask.

She shrugs. "I love preparing for my family. This is much smaller than the one we'll have on Christmas when we have both sides of the family over. And you, of course, are always welcome."

"This house will be like a zoo," Martin says when

he returns with the pies—chocolate peanut butter and pumpkin—and cheesecake. They're all smaller portions of the ones I assume she's going to make for Christmas Day. "I'd stay away if I were you."

Clarice swats at her husband. "Hey now! You told me yourself that you enjoy the chaos. That's why we invite both sides of the family over on Christmas Day and spend Christmas Eve just the four of us."

Martin smiles at his wife. "I know. I was only teasing. The chaos is good…for a time. In a way, it kind of makes December 26th a very special day in itself."

Clarice laughs and swats at him again. "Don't listen to him, Eddie. Please, I hope you seriously consider celebrating with us on Christmas. I would hate to see you by yourself next door while our house is filled with people." She shakes her head. "I wouldn't be able to celebrate properly myself if I knew you were over there all alone."

"Don't worry about me," I tell her as I accept a plate of each dessert from Blake. "I'm used to being on my own."

"But that doesn't mean it's right," Clarice pushes. "You know, you need to get out more. You spend a lot of time alone."

I take a bite of the chocolate peanut butter pie and savor the rich flavor. Waving my fork at her, I finish chewing and say, "Well, if you consider that half of my friends are married with kids—and grandkids—of their own and the other half are dead, then that kind of ties me up."

Ryan snorts laughter at my directness as he cuts himself a piece of pie.

Clarice's eyes widen. "I'm sure that's not true. What about people you used to know?"

"You mean my ex-wife?" I ask. "Betty and I were only married a couple years. She moved on pretty quickly after me, so I don't think she'd be up for me crashing her Christmas—or any other day of her life."

Now it's Blake's turn to laugh.

I smirk, enjoying giving the boys some comedic relief.

"Surely you couldn't have gone your whole life without any friends. And I'm sure some of them would love to see you."

My thoughts immediately go to Collette, whom I haven't seen since high school when we broke up. I've never loved anyone quite like her. At this moment, like I often do, I wonder if she ever thinks of me. Thinks of what our life could've been like if things had turned out differently.

But, I'll never see her again.

"You know what you should do?" Clarice waves her fork at me now. "You should join Facebook."

Both of her boys groan.

"Mom!" Ryan says.

"What?" she asks innocently.

"Facebook is so lame!" Blake adds. "It's for, like, *old* people."

"Apparently the boys have forgotten their audience," Martin jokes to me.

I smile. "Apparently so."

"I'm serious!" Clarice says. "I've reconnected with so many people that I've completely forgotten about. Now I see pictures of their kids, follow them on vacations, and even celebrate job changes and things like that. It's a great thing."

"I don't know, Clarice," I tell her.

She apparently doesn't hear me, as she's left her half-eaten pie at her spot on the table to retrieve her laptop and her reading glasses. She takes the seat next to me and opens her computer. The glow of the screen illuminates her face and she slides on her glasses as she finger-pecks the keyboard.

Over the next twenty minutes, despite my objections, Clarice gets me set up with an account, which includes taking a picture of me that I can't say is the best one ever taken of me, but my best is years in the past.

As she gets the app downloaded on my phone, I notice that the rest of her family has quietly picked up the traces of dinner from the dining room and retreated to the various corners of their house. Martin washes the dishes in the kitchen while the boys sit in front of the TV in the living room.

"Clarice, I appreciate you trying to help me out, but—"

"Here." She hands me back my phone. "I've connected your account to your contacts list. Now, Facebook will suggest people you might know so you can add them as friends. In the meantime, let's look up some people from your past. Who was your best friend growing up?"

I sigh. "Paul Dombrowski."

"Who?" she asks.

I repeat his last name slower and spell it out for her. Within a few seconds, I'm staring at a picture of him. Paul is someone I lost touch with back when I was in the service. And yet now, I'm staring at a picture of him. The son-of-a-gun looks old. But then, so do I. "Wow, is that really him?"

Clarice smiles beside me, satisfied with herself. "Mm-hmm. You can message him here, search through his pictures here, and see what he's posted down here."

I scroll through some of my old friend's pictures, amazed that I'm getting a glimpse into his life. Something I haven't been a part of in close to fifty years.

"Pretty amazing, isn't it?" Clarice beams.

"I'll say."

"Who else do you want to look up?"

I glance up at the clock and see that it's just after seven. "Oh, I need to get home. I'll have to look up some names from my handwritten address book back at the house." I stand and begin my exit. "You know, the old school way."

Clarice follows me to the door. "Be sure to reach out to people. Otherwise, this whole thing is pointless."

I nod. "I promise. I will. Thanks for dinner."

"Of course. You're more than welcome anytime. And I want you to consider coming here for Christmas."

"Thanks for that invitation, but I think it's best that it's just you and your family. I'll be okay." I pull on my coat and my boots. I give her a wave as I walk out into the cold.

I don't have to look behind me to know that Clarice is watching me through the window until I get into my house. Even though I'm only sixty-seven, she treats me like I'm an ancient old beast.

I suppose her judgment isn't too far off.

Inside, I kick off my boots, throw my coat on the hook, and flick on the living room light so that I can wave to Clarice from inside the house. She doesn't tell me she's watching me, but I know that she looks for the lights to flick on to know that everything is okay.

I take a seat on the couch and pull out my phone. The first name I search for is Collette Hopkins.

Within seconds, I see her face staring back at me. The one I've dreamt about for the last fifty years. The one I've longed for. The one that I wish I would've held onto tighter.

I'm glad I'm alone when I search for her because the sight of her face brings tears to my eyes. My one true love, finally within my reach again.

December 22nd
Collette

❄ ❄ ❄

*I*ve started every Sunday of my life at church. It's what my parents instilled in me and, now that I'm a grown adult, I find comfort in these traditions. To me, it's nice to have a refresher of what it means to be a good person, even if that definition is changing with the times.

So when I step into the church on the last Sunday of Advent, and I'm greeted with the beautiful Christmas decorations and hear the wonderful music played on the organ, I feel at home. At peace.

I sidle up in a pew beside Maureen and her husband, Henry. "Good morning! Room for one more?"

"Of course, Collette, there's always room for you."

Maureen nudges her husband to move over and creates a space for me.

"Isn't it beautiful in here?" I coo as I pull off my jacket. "It fills my heart with so much warmth."

Maureen nods. "I know. And, honestly, the beauty of this building is one of the reasons that Isaac and Tori have decided to get married here."

I smile politely. "How long have they been together now?"

"It's five years this Christmas! It's about time that they're finally tying the knot."

"Seems like you've been talking about them forever." The snipe is uncalled for and I tell myself to behave. Maureen is excited about her son's wedding. No wonder she talks about it nonstop, as if it were her *own* wedding.

"That's what I've been telling them! You know, they first got together at Christmas time. It was for the Batavia Holiday Choir…"

As my friend recounts the story I've heard a million times before, I let my mind drift. It's the least I can do to keep my snark to myself. And besides, Mass will be starting soon.

I hum along quietly to the music as the rest of the congregation files in. When the music stops and everyone stands up to sing, that's when Maureen finally wraps up her story.

"Anyway, they've been a match made in heaven ever since."

I wouldn't go so far as to say they were a match made *in heaven*. At least, not by my mother's standards. Isaac and Tori have been dating for five years and living together for four of them. They don't call it "shaking up in sin" for nothing.

Then again, I'm not one to talk with the things I've done in my past. I was young once. I understand. Too bad my parents didn't.

When Mass is over, I file out into the aisle, but linger as Maureen chats about what she still needs to do to get ready for the holiday. When she moves on, then it's Nancy Slater coming over to say hi and give me a hug, as if we didn't just see each other yesterday.

I chat with as many friends as I can. Typically, I'm the last one out of the church. Sunday is my least-busy day of the week for me. The library is closed, and all of my other volunteer organizations are closed on Sundays too. If it wasn't for church, I would have no opportunity to socialize.

As the crowd noticeably thins out, I finally decide it's time to go home. Maybe finish that Debbie Macomber book I tried to read yesterday before succumbing to a nap. Or maybe take a nap and *then* read. And I wouldn't mind baking a few more cookies for the neighbors as a thank you for helping me with the snow so far this winter.

But as I make my way to the back of the church, all of my good intentions come to a screeching halt when I see who is standing in the doorway as the crowd moves around him to exit.

Eddie Marshall.

I stop dead in my tracks and have to reach for a nearby pew to steady myself. All of the air has suddenly disappeared from my lungs.

"Is it really you?" I ask.

With tears in his eyes, he nods. "It is."

Without another moment's hesitation, we both run to each other, colliding in a long-awaited embrace. My lips find his and I can't seem to squeeze him tight enough.

It's like we're teenagers again. Kissing and holding each other, no matter who is watching.

When we finally tear away from one another enough so that we can look into each other's eyes, both of us are crying.

"I've missed you so much," I tell him. My hands run up and down his back, feeling him but not necessarily believing that he's here, right in front of me.

"Not as much as I've missed you." He caresses my face and it's as if we're teenagers again.

"But…I don't understand. How are you here? Where did you find me? I thought you might've…" I shake my head, not able to bring myself to speak the word: *died*. "I just figured you had moved on."

He shakes his head. "Never. I could never move on. Not from you, Collette. Never from you. I still love you just as much as I did when we were kids."

"I feel the same way." I smile and wipe away the tears from my eyes. "Eddie, I never stopped loving you. It's always been you."

"I can't believe it's been—"

"Fifty years," I finish for him. The last time I saw him is still vivid in my mind. The intervention both of our parents held. The way they forbade us from seeing each other. How I was shipped off to my aunt's house in Syracuse until—

"Maybe we should get some coffee?" he suggests. "We have a lot to catch up on, and this may take a while."

"It certainly will." Arm linked with his, I start to lead him to the door. Everyone else has cleared out already. At the door, I stop. "Oh. Wait. It's Sunday."

"Still sharp as a tack," he jokes.

I swat at him. How quickly we've returned back to our playful banter. "No, I meant that everything is closed."

"Oh." Eddie's shoulders sag.

"You know what? Let's just go back to my house. We can have all the coffee we want and nobody will kick us out."

"Are you sure that's not too forward?" He turns my hand over in his and studies it.

I squeeze his hand and tug on it to get his attention. "We just made out in a church and you're worried about what we might do in private? Besides, with our history, there's nothing too forward."

"I MADE A full pot because this is going to take a while." I set the pot on an oven mitt on the coffee table, then retreat to the kitchen to retrieve the two full coffee mugs.

"Are you sure I can't help with anything?" Eddie asks from his perch on the couch.

"No, just make yourself comfortable."

"Your house is beautiful." He looks around at it.

"Thank you." I try to take it in with fresh eyes. I've been fortunate to own it for most of my adult life, meaning that I've been able to retain much of the historic charm of the small colonial. "The first few years were rough, but with no family, the money didn't need to be spent on anything else, so…"

Eddie nods. "I know what you mean. I've moved a few times, but it hasn't always been the financial burden on me as it is for some people because it's always been just me. Well, except for that short time that I was married."

My eyes shoot down to my coffee cradled in my hands. "So you did marry then?" My voice is small. I try to keep the hurt out of it, but it's impossible to completely conceal my feelings. Especially after I just mauled him in church.

"For a bit." He reaches for my hand and I meet his eyes. "It never felt like it did with you, Collette. I thought maybe it would. Maybe if we were married, I would start to feel a deeper sense of love for her. That my commitment would make me feel more for her. But it didn't. It couldn't. Especially when I was constantly comparing her to you in my mind and, no offense to her, but nobody could *ever* compare to you, Collette."

I offer him a smile. I'm still a little hurt that he had married, but we weren't a part of each other's lives then. He deserved to try and make himself happy.

"After my wife and I divorced, I swore off ever trying to get married again—or even trying to find someone to spend my time with," he says. "Not when I was still so deeply in love with you."

I squeeze his hand back. "And I still love you. Even after all these years."

"Even though I've put on some weight and have gone gray?"

"*Especially* with your age." I lean forward and stroke his face. "Besides, it's not like I'm one to talk. Look at me."

"I am. You're as beautiful as ever."

I bark out a laugh as I bring the mug to my lips. "I'm no prom queen, but I'll take the compliment."

"What about you?" he asks. "Have you ever married?"

"Nope. Never really looked. I had a few boyfriends here and there, but nothing that lasted longer than a year." My eyes meet his again. "Does that make you happy?"

He shrugs, suppressing a smirk. "Can't say it makes me *un*happy."

"I spent thirty-four years working as an English teacher up the street." I gesture in the direction of the Catholic high school where I was previously employed. "The men I worked with were either married or ordained."

Eddie laughs. "Kind of narrows the dating pool, doesn't it?"

"Just a bit. Before I retired, I would spend my free time lesson planning, visiting my sister, or playing cards with the girls."

"And now that you're retired?"

"I'm too busy volunteering. Besides that, I've gone this long on my own, why would I be looking for companionship now?"

"So you don't want to get back together?" he asks.

I hook my eyebrow and look over at him. "As far as I'm concerned, that kiss in the church basically sealed the deal."

He smiles. "Not officially, but it did seem pretty binding, didn't it?"

"What about you? What have you been up to for the last fifty years, besides swearing off marriage?"

"I worked as a mechanic for a long time. Just retired last year, actually. I still tinker with my car from time to time with the neighbor boys. That Mustang I had when I was a teenager?"

My eyes light up. "You still have that!?"

He smiles. "Of course I do! Reminds me of you."

I blush. "If those walls could talk."

"More like, if that *back seat* could talk."

I swat at him again and let out a giggle. I haven't laughed like that since I was a kid. A teenager. Seventeen. The last time I was with Eddie.

"Nowadays I'm mostly the neighborhood handyman." He shrugs. "It keeps me busy. Gets me out of the house. Makes me feel needed. For a bit, at least. Sometimes, I feel like the neighbors ask me for help because they feel bad for me."

My face sours. "Oh, I'm sure that's not true. You've always known your way around your tools. I'm sure your neighbors recognize that and value your expertise."

"Maybe." He downs the rest of his coffee.

I reach for the pot and pour him a refill, then refill my own.

We spend the next hour reminiscing of our time together as teenagers. Laughing at stories that we've both loved—and, sometimes, remembered differently. The time Eddie and I snuck back into the school after his football game and made out. Or how some of his teammates used to call us EdCo, since we were always together. Or the first time we met, back in junior high, when Eddie and his family first moved to Batavia. We had four classes together, and spent every possible moment in each other's presence. It wasn't until he asked me to the Winter Formal that we started going steady.

It's amazing how quickly our banter has returned. How fast we've slipped right back into being Eddie and Collette, the "it" couple.

From what I heard when I returned from my aunt's house, after Eddie had already moved away to enter the service, everyone was shocked that we had split up. Rumors flew, sure, but I never commented on any of them. And my real friends never asked.

Eddie's parents moved away shortly after he entered the service. That only fueled more rumors around town. That was one of the reasons why I opted to work at a private school instead of a public one. Gossip and rumors didn't always cross. Or maybe the people around me were just being polite. Either way, the gossip died down and I was able to move on with my life.

Without Eddie.

"Oh my, we've finished a whole pot of coffee," I say when I notice that the pot is empty.

"We sure have. Do you mind if I use your restroom?"

"Of course not. Around the corner on the right. I'll make another pot."

"Better make it tea," he warns me. "If I have anymore coffee, I'll be up all night."

Five minutes later, I bring our teas out into the living room, where Eddie has returned. He's standing at the Christmas tree, looking at the ornaments. He extends his hand out to one in particular. Over his shoulder I see that it's the stained glass lily.

"That's for someone *else* that I haven't stopped thinking about over the last fifty years," I tell him. "Our daughter."

Eddie turns to face me and pulls his lips together. "So you had a girl, then. I've always wondered about that."

I lead him back to the couch, where I pull my legs up under me. "I wanted to name her Lillian Grace." I suck in a deep breath, finally allowing myself to recall the memories I had shoved down for so long. "Of course, the mother isn't allowed to name the baby when they're giving them up for adoption."

He joins me on the couch and reaches for my hand. "I just wish I had had a chance to meet her. With all due respect, our parents were very cruel in that regard."

I nod, remembering how Eddie and I had been forced apart when I became pregnant. Now, so many decades later, I understand what they were trying to do, and I only hope that it occurred to them the pain that they had put me through—put us both through—as a result of their actions.

"Oh, she was beautiful, Eddie." My voice cracks and I wipe a tear away from my eyes. The memory of that innocent, perfect little baby in my arms is still fresh in my mind. "I hated giving her up. *Hated* it." I shake my head. "But, truth be told, it was the right choice. We *were* too young to be parents."

Eddie nods. "We were kids. I did a lot of growing up in the service. If I hadn't gone, I would've missed out on all of the experiences I had. And if I had gone, I would've left you alone with the baby."

"I held resentment against my parents for a long time," I tell him. "The way they dictated my life. Tore apart the ones I loved the most. They didn't understand just how deeply we loved each other."

"It was a different time," he says. "Back in the early seventies, an unwed teenaged pregnancy was *very* taboo. Our parents were from a different generation. To them, it was just puppy love between us."

I suck in another shaky breath and reach for his hand again for comfort. "I know. And I've forgiven them for being a product of their generation. Lord knows I have my own views and morals that probably differ from the kids growing up today."

"Yeah. Me too."

We grow silent as the daylight outside gets dimmer, made worse by the falling snow. It drifts slowly from the sky to the ground, creating a sense of peace and calm as it blankets the world.

"I wonder where Lily is now," I say in a quiet voice. "I wonder what our lives would be like if we hadn't been forced apart. I wonder how differently things would've turned out."

Eddie meets my eyes and squeezes my hand. "I wonder the same things too. But, at least you and I have come back together now. It's not perfect, but better late than never, right?"

I smile, then lean forward and kiss him.

He wraps an arm around me and we settle into the couch together, watching the snow fall through the window.

❅ ❅ ❅

THE HALLMARK MOVIE finishes playing and I sit up on the couch. My eyelids are heavy and my old body feels tired from staying up later than I normally do.

Eddie starts to stir from his slumber beside me. I had been laying on him and my movement rouses him.

"It's late." I point the remote at the TV and turn it off. "We should get some sleep."

Eddie shifts so that he's sitting up, then with some effort, he lifts himself up to his feet.

Without realizing it, I step toward him and into his embrace again. Our movements easy. Relaxed. Natural.

He kisses me and I wrap my arms around him. This feels like a dream, being back in his arms. I can hardly believe that it's happening.

"I don't think I'm driving home tonight," he says, placing a quick kiss on my lips. We can hardly keep our hands off each other.

"No, I don't think you are."

"So then I'll have to stay here."

Another kiss.

"I'd like that."

"So what are my options? Am I bunking it on the couch or…?"

He doesn't need to finish his question. It's something I've been considering since we settled in for the movie. The passion between us is unquestionable. And I think the fifty years we've waited has been penance enough.

Still. I want our first time back together to be special. Monumental. Not hurried and rushed while we're both half asleep.

But I don't want to disappoint him, either.

I kiss him once, then say, "Well, you have two options. I have a guest bedroom upstairs. Or the room *beside* the guest bedroom…where I'll be sleeping."

He smirks. "That's a tough choice."

I look up at him. "I figured you'd use the opportunity to make a joke."

"This doesn't seem funny."

I rest my head against his chest, glad that he's taking this seriously. That he's showing that our reunion means something to him.

"I would love to take the room beside the guest room. Trust me. But I think, for tonight, at least, I should take the guest bedroom."

A mix of emotions flood through me. Relief. Hurt. Desire. It's all there. And yet, I know that it's the right choice. We only reunited this morning.

"Okay." I give him a smile to let him know that it's truly okay, then give him another kiss for good measure. "Let me show you to your room, then."

DECEMBER 23RD
Eddie

❄ ❄ ❄

I fumble around in Collette's kitchen looking for the coffee mugs. Just as I'm about to give up, I find them in the cabinet on the end. I pull out two, then set about making a pot of coffee.

As the morning brew begins to percolate, I poke through Collette's fridge and decide that she has enough to make her breakfast. We can stop at the grocery store later so I can replace whatever I use. I normally don't like taking such liberties, but not only do I feel like my blood sugar is dropping, but I think it would be a nice gesture. And I want to do something nice for her.

Fifteen minutes later, with the omelettes sizzling on the stove, Collette steps into the kitchen. "Morning." She ties her bathrobe tighter around herself.

"Morning, beautiful." I lean in and kiss her. Coffee for two, breakfast, and morning kisses. How quickly I've been domesticated!

The toaster pops and I pull away long enough to pull the toast out and start to butter it. "The coffee should be ready."

She walks over to pour herself a cup. "Oh, you're spoiling me."

"Sit down." I motion to the small kitchen table. "I'll bring everything to you."

She finishes fixing herself a cup of coffee, then does as I ask and takes a seat at the table. "How'd you sleep?" She takes a careful sip of her coffee, then sets it down on the table in front of her, cradling it in her hands.

I turn the burner off on the stove, grab two plates, and dish out the food. "Not bad. Would've slept better with you in my arms."

Last night we had both toyed with the idea of going to bed together. Clearly, we both wanted it, but our parents' admonishing for premarital sex when we were younger was heavy on my mind with all the talk of the past. Apparently, those scars still run deep.

Collette gives me a wry grin over the rim of her coffee mug. "I agree. But, it's probably best that we wait for the rush of this reunion to settle before we do anything rash."

I nod along, even though I don't know what "rash" decisions she could be talking about. Less than twenty-four hours ago we hadn't even known the other was alive and well, and now we had practically moved in together.

At this stage of my life, if I don't grab what I want quickly, I know it'll disappear only too fast.

"Do you plan on staying for Christmas?" she asks.

I shrug. "To be honest, I've kind of forgotten about the holiday, after all the excitement yesterday."

"It's in two days, Eddie. My house is lit up so much you can practically see it from across town. *How* could you forget about it?"

"I'm more interested in you." And I am. As she eats, I watch her simple beauty. Nothing about her is putting on anything for show, and yet her body moves with such ease and confidence that she just exudes strength and allure.

"Well, Christmas is usually a quiet day for me here," she says, "but Christmas *Eve* is pretty busy, what with catching up with friends in the morning for breakfast, then going to help out with the children's choir at the church, and, of course, Christmas Eve Mass…"

On and on she goes about the major holiday that is nearly upon us, but all I'm focused on is pinpointing the traces of the girl I used to know when I was seventeen, mixed in with the woman she's become over the last fifty years. While she has matured so much, her true essence is still the same.

Still the same girl I fell in love with.

"Eddie, are you listening to me?" she asks, which pulls me out of my stupor.

I look down and notice that both of our plates are empty. "Oh. Um. Yes. Christmas. How great." I pile our plates on top of each other and carry them to the sink. "Why don't you go upstairs and take a shower while I clean up these dishes?"

"Okay, now I *know* you're spoiling me." She comes up and wraps her arms around me from behind as I stand at the sink. "I'm so glad you came back to me. You're proof that God is real. My prayers have been answered."

I turn to face her, wrapping her in my arms as well. We kiss, then I say, "I love you." I'll never get tired of telling her that.

"I love you too. Always have. Never stopped." She kisses me again. Deeper this time.

The temptation that we felt last night returns as the lust between us builds. Finally, I pull away. "Okay, I'm going to clean up the kitchen. Otherwise, I think we're likely to get busy on the kitchen floor, and I know that's not the way either of us want to reunite."

"No, I want it to be special." She offers me a playful wave as she leaves the room.

I watch the doorway for a moment after she's gone, allowing myself to cool down from the moment. Then I begin cleaning the kitchen.

WITH THE KITCHEN clean, and after running out to my car to retrieve something important, I find myself back in the living room, where I spend some uninterrupted time inspecting more of Collette's Christmas ornaments on the tree. I'm stuck on the first one that catches my eye, though. The lily ornament, placed in memory of our baby.

Alone, I allow the painful memories and regrets that I've pushed away my whole life come back. I wish I had been able to raise her. Walk her down the aisle at her wedding. Put a Band-Aid on her knee when she fell off her bike as a girl. Taught her how to stand up for herself.

Most of all, I regret not being able to get to know her. To witness her personal growth from baby to little girl to teenager to woman. To watch as she goes after the things she wants in life. To celebrate her victories with her.

I wonder what she's like. She has to be at least fifty. I bet she's aged gracefully, like Collette. I wonder if Lily went to college, what kind of job she has. If she's is married. If she has any kids—or grandkids. If she did, that would make me a grandfather, or even a great-grandfather! Somehow, I don't feel like I'm old enough for that. It's definitely something I never imagined I would be.

But since I've reunited with Collette, my mind is

running rampant with all of the possibilities that suddenly exist for me. Things I never thought I'd get to experience. Love. Pillow talk. Anniversaries. Being able to say, "My wife."

That's a big one, and about the only thing I enjoyed when I was married. Calling someone my wife felt like I wasn't alone in the world. But the title never quite fit with my first wife.

The stairs creak as Collette comes down after her shower. I turn and use the wall to help lower myself to the floor on one knee. My high school class ring, still cold from being out in my car, is held between my fingers.

She stops in her tracks when she sees it and clutches her heart. "Oh, Eddie."

"I know this might seem…unexpected," I start. "We only found each other again yesterday. But if there's one thing I'm sure of, it's how much I love you. And I know you love me too. We may have gotten a late start at this in life, but better late than never. I love you, Collette, and I am so happy that we found each other again. The only way I can be happier than I am at this moment is if I have you as my wife. Will you marry me?"

She chokes back a sob. "Oh, Eddie," she says again. "Of course, I'll marry you! The answer was always yes!"

As she steps forward, I slide the ring on her finger. It's a perfect fit. My hands as a teenager were skinny and lanky. Now, after years of working with them, my fingers are fat with callouses. The ring hasn't fit me in years. I take that to mean that it was always meant for Collette's finger.

She takes my face in her hands and kisses me from my kneeling position.

I break the kiss. "Not to ruin our special moment, but my joints aren't what they used to be. I could use a hand up."

Collette's head falls back as she lets out a laugh. "Yes, of course." She lends me her hand and, with great effort, I'm back on my feet.

"Thanks. Probably won't be the last time you'll have to help me off the floor."

She slides easily into my arms. "I'm looking forward to helping you up for the rest of our lives."

"Which is hopefully a long time since we're going to be old geezer newlyweds."

Another playful slap in my direction. "Oh shush. We're not that old!"

"Old enough to have a middle-aged daughter!" I blurt. It's an attempt at a joke, but judging by the sad look on Collette's face, she doesn't find the humor in it. "Collette, I'm sorry. I didn't mean to bring up bad feelings. I shouldn't have said that."

"No, it's not that." Her eyes drift off, even though she's still wrapped in my arms. "It's just that, I can't marry you."

"What?" My heart feels like it's shattered into a million pieces.

She shakes her head. "Not without finding our daughter first. Now that you and I have reconnected, I can't help but feel like there's still a part of me missing. A part of *us* missing."

I nod. "I know what you mean. I feel the same way. I love that we're together, but it just doesn't *quite* feel like it's enough. Not without knowing where our Lily is."

She smiles. "Is that what we're calling her, then?"

"Until we know her real name, why not?" I give her a peck. "It's time we reunite our family. Long overdue, actually."

Collette slides her hand in mine. I feel the ring on her finger as her hands entwine with mine. She's drawn by it too. "You know, when we were first dating, I wanted nothing more than to wear your class ring." She chuckles. "Back then, it was a status symbol for girls to wear their guy's class ring. To show off that they were taken."

"And now it's yours. Where it belongs."

"And I don't give a damn who sees," she adds. "All I care about is being with you. But we can't get married until we find Lily."

"So let's go find her." The thought just occurs to me. "Today. Let's go."

Collette brightens. "But where would we even begin?"

"Well, where did you give her up for adoption back in 1974?"

She breathes in a heavy breath. I can tell that it takes a lot of effort for her to recall that painful part of her life. The part that I wasn't allowed to be a part of. That guilt I will carry around with me for the rest of my life.

"Our Lady of Victory Unwed Mothers in Lackawanna," she finally says. "I gave birth in Syracuse where I was staying with my aunt. My parents came after I gave birth and…" She sighs again. "…and they were the ones who dropped her off. My mother had a connection with a priest in Lackawanna. She said Lily would be in good hands." She shakes her head. "I still regret not taking her myself."

I squeeze her tight, resting my head on top of hers. We sit, quietly, for a while, as we both digest the painful memories that we have spent so long trying to bury and move on from.

"Then let's start there," I say after a long while. "They have to have a record of babies that came and went. At the very least, they'll have to have a connection to the adoptive family."

"It's a long shot," she says.

"But one that's worth shooting," I say. We both know we'd regret not even trying to look for her.

Collette smiles. "I'd like that."

"All right, then let's go. We just need to stop at my

house so I can shower and change." I pick at my shirt, which is wrinkled and probably smells a bit like sweat. "I wasn't expecting to spend the night."

She smirks. "Sorry about that."

I kiss her. "There's nothing to apologize for. I had a great time."

"WHAT DO YOU think she looks like?" Collette asks me on the way back to my house. She's inspecting the gem on my class ring. It fits perfectly on her finger.

"Who?"

"Lily. Or whatever her name is. Her real name. What do you think that is?"

I shrug. "I don't know. And I have no idea what she looks like, either. But I do know this for certain: with your genes, I'm sure she's beautiful."

Collette plays with the zipper on her jacket. "That's what I would like to think too, but what if she's not? What if her adoptive parents were horrible to her? What if she fell into drugs or an abusive marriage or hasn't found something in her life that makes her happy and gives her purpose?"

I take her hand and hold it on the center console while I drive. "Honey, you're letting your mind run rampant with worry."

"How could I not? Now that I've found you, I

can't help but feel like a part of me is still missing. If I'm being honest, I've always felt like that a bit, but until yesterday, I figured that finding our daughter was never even a possibility. Now, it's like this whole previous life I've lived has been unlocked. But I've lived so long without it, that it's a little scary."

I bring her hand to my lips and kiss the back of it. "How about you think of it this way instead: Lily probably went to a couple who couldn't have kids on their own, for whatever reason. And, thanks to our sacrifice — really, *yours* — that couple was finally able to have the family that they've always dreamed of. We made *their* family complete."

Collette squeezes my hand back. "I like that idea. I hope you're right. I just wish we would've been able to raise her ourselves."

I nod and swallow the lump in my throat. "I know. Me too."

❄ ❄ ❄

IN MY DRIVEWAY, I come around to Collette's side of the car to open it for her. I've missed out on years of chivalry, I have a lot of time to make up for. Not that she *needs* the helping hand, but she definitely deserves it.

"Thank you," she says as she allows me to help her out of the car and into the cold. She looks up and down the street. "This looks like a nice neighborhood."

My house is in the middle of one of the many subdivisions in Cheektowaga. Even though the houses are all cookie-cutter, the friendly neighbors help make this place feel like home.

"It is. The neighbors are —"

"Eddie!" Clarice calls from next door. As if she knew that I had just about to talk about my neighbors. "Where have you been?" She's bundled up in her jacket, but Martin's boots, which haven't been tied. Clearly, she had been looking for me out the window. "When you didn't come home last night, I was worried sick!"

I can't help but smile and blush a little. Thankfully, in the cold, my cheeks are already red. "Clarice, this is Collette. Collette, this is my neighbor, Clarice."

The two women shake hands.

"Nice to meet you," Collette offers with a friendly smile.

"You too," Clarice says, then turns back to me, waiting for my answer.

"Nothing to worry about," I say. "Everything is fine. Better than fine, actually. I used that book face thing to find the love of my life." I hook an arm around Collette. "We've decided to get married."

Clarice's eyebrows raise in concern. "Married?"

I nod. "Yep. All thanks to you!"

"Me?"

"If you hadn't showed me how to use that face

booker, then I never would've been able to track down Collette!"

Clarice recovers from her shock and clears her throat. "Collette, would you mind giving me and Eddie some time alone to chat?"

We can all tell that Clarice is not happy by the news, but none of us speak to it just yet.

I pull out my keys from my pocket, find the one for the front door, and hand it to Collette. "Go inside and make yourself at home. I'll be in in a sec."

"It was nice meeting you," Collette offers to my neighbor, who smiles and waves politely as she watches her disappear into the house.

When it's just the two of us in the driveway, Clarice turns back to me. "Eddie, are you sure that you want to get married? You just met this woman!"

I shake my head. "That's where you're wrong. I've known her since grade school. We dated as teenagers before…um, before I went into the service. It's been fifty years and I haven't stopped thinking about her. She hasn't stopped thinking about me, either. Getting married was the easiest decision I've ever made."

"Then what difference does it make if you wait? At least until you've reconnected a little bit longer?"

I put my hands on Clarice's shoulders. "Thank you for your concern, but you can't change my mind. Collette has always been the one that got away. I'm not going to let her get away any longer."

Clarice sighs, still not liking the idea. "Eddie, I don't want you to rush into anything."

I give her a look. "Clarice, I'm sixty-seven years old. There's nothing I'm *rushing into* anymore." I give her a kiss on the top of the head, then turn to go back into the house. Back to the woman I've been waiting fifty years to find again.

DECEMBER 23RD
Collette

***

As I watch Eddie and Clarice talk through the window, I know that I am the topic of conversation. Clarice did nothing to hide her discomfort at the idea of me and Eddie together, which seems to dim my excitement about the long-awaited proposal this morning.

To get my mind off of it, I make my way to Eddie's kitchen and take a seat at the table, where I call up Nancy Slater.

"Nancy? It's Collette." Even as the words leave my lips, I know they're pointless. Old habits die hard, especially when I've grown up without caller ID.

"Collette, how are you?"

"I'm doing okay. Listen, I don't have a lot of time to

talk. I just wanted to give you a buzz to see if you'd be willing to go to church and help Maureen clean up from the bake sale. I told her I'd come and help sort dishes."

"Sort dishes? Didn't folks just use those disposable foil pans?"

"Not all of them," I say. "Some people just made things in whatever pan they had in the house."

Nancy scoffs. "It's not like the disposable ones are expensive! You can get a whole pack of them at Walmart!"

"Some people probably didn't have time to go out and buy the disposable ones, but they still wanted to help." Sensing that the conversation has gone off the rails, I bring it back on track. "Can you help Maureen or not?"

"I haven't prepared anything, but I suppose I can stop by."

I smirk. "You don't need to bring any food, Nancy. It's possible to help out *without* feeding the other volunteers."

She sighs. "I know, I just like to feed my friends. I suppose I can pick up some muffins from Books & Bakes on the way. Hey, why can't you help?"

"Um…something's come up."

"You've said *that*, I want to know *what*. Where are you?"

There's no getting out of this. "I'm in Buffalo—well, Cheektowaga, really."

"What are you doing *out there*?"

Some people think that Buffalo and Batavia are a million miles apart. It's only about a thirty minute commute, depending on where you're going.

"Um, well, yesterday I reconnected with an old boyfriend—"

"Is that who you were kissing yesterday in church?"

My cheeks redden and I'm glad I'm talking to her on the phone so she can't see. How many other people saw us? Then again, who cares? I clear my throat. "Uh, yes."

"Collette! It's about time you found someone!"

Like Nancy is one to talk. Ever since her husband passed away, she has had no interest in finding companionship. Not that I blame her. If, heaven forbid, Eddie were to pass away, I would feel the same way.

"Yes, well, we've decided to get married and— you know what? It's a long story. I'll tell you and the girls all about it later. The reason I called is that I won't be able to help Maureen like I'd planned. You said you can?"

Nancy is quiet on the other end of the line. Something that's very unusual, especially with such juicy gossip.

When the silence drags on, I say, "Nancy? What's wrong?"

"Well," she says in an exhale. "This, um, *news*

makes me a little nervous. I just want you to be careful."

"I know. And I am."

"Are you sure you're ready to *marry* him?" Nancy asks. "I mean, it's been—how long has it been?"

"Fifty years." My eyes widen as it suddenly hits me just how long it's been. How had we gotten so old? How did we let so many years slip by?

"Fifty years! Collette, you need to slow down. Date him for a little bit before you—"

"I've never been more sure of anything in my life, Nancy. I can't wait to introduce Eddie to all of you girls after Christmas. Now, please make sure you meet Maureen by eleven. Otherwise, she'll get cranky—you know how she can be."

Nancy doesn't laugh at my joke. "Collette, please be careful."

"I will. Thanks for helping me out."

When I hang up the phone, Eddie steps into the kitchen and finds me examining the ring on my finger. I used to see it on his back in high school. Funny how it fits me so well now, all these years later.

"Is there something else you need to get to?" he asks.

I shake my head. "No. Just freeing my schedule to be with you." I stand and wrap my arms around him.

He kisses me. "I love you."

"I love you too."

"Now, I need to go shower so we can go find Lily." He pulls away, then motions to the kitchen. "Make yourself at home. I'll be as quick as I can." He disappears around the corner.

In his absence, I take the opportunity to look around his house. On the fridge he has several pictures of different kids held up by magnets. I study them, but can't seem to place Eddie's connection to them.

A part of me wonders, if things had been different, if Eddie and I had been together all along, if these faces would mean something to me. Would I look at them fondly, as Eddie presumably does? As it is, these faces are of perfect strangers.

I step into the living room to look for more pictures of people that I might recognize, but what I *don't* see stops me.

There isn't a shred of Christmas decoration at all in the house. No tree. No garland. No lights. Not even a wreath on the front door, now that I think about it.

As I inspect further, I don't see any other pictures of anyone hanging on his walls, or set on his furniture in the living room. Those pictures on the fridge must've been from Christmas cards. The cards clearly went right in the trash when they came in the mail.

Who does Eddie have in his life? Even though I don't have any family, I at least have my best friends, whom I see regularly, and have pictures of the group of us throughout my house from over the years. Eddie's house is a stark reflection of his lonely life, and that thought makes my heart hurt.

Of course, Eddie might have best friends and just doesn't have any pictures of them. Maybe he has a crew, like mine, that are thick as thieves. I wonder what they're like. Will I like them? Will I be able to blend right in with them? Will he be able to blend in with *my* friends? How are we going to merge our two lives together, this late in our lives? We're both old and stuck in our ways. We've both lived alone for all of our adult lives. Do I even know *how* to live with someone else? That thought scares me a bit, but also excites me to figure it out.

Eddie comes back into the living room fifteen minutes later, showered and dressed. "Sorry that took so long."

I shake my head. "You were quick." My voice is flat.

"What's wrong?" he comes and sits next to me on the couch.

"Your house is empty."

He looks around, confused.

"There's no decorations up. I know you're alone, but doesn't it make you feel happy to celebrate Christmas, even on your own?"

He shrugs. "I guess I never really saw the point in it."

"Oh." My face darkens. "That makes me sad."

Eddie takes my hand. "Well, yesterday was a wake-up call for me. Not only did I find you again, but I saw your beautifully-decorated house. I understand what you see now. I want the same thing. Only, now neither of us will be alone anymore. Next year, you and I will deck the halls to the max."

I laugh. "Okay. Deal."

"So what do you say?" he asks. "Are we ready to go track down our daughter?" He starts to get up, but I pull him back down.

"Just one more thing," I say. "Are we crazy?"

"Crazy in love."

I swat at his arm. "I'm serious. Are we crazy for all of this? For coming together so quickly, getting married, trying to find the daughter we gave up fifty years ago? I mean, it's obvious your neighbor has some opinions about it."

"Who, Clarice?" Eddie peers out the window. "She has an opinion on everything. Thinks that I'm one of her kids that she can boss around. But I'm a grown man who doesn't listen to someone old enough to be my daughter." He shakes his head. "Don't worry about her."

"It's not just her, though," I say. "I called my friend a little while ago and she just kept telling me to be careful. If they both think this is all too fast, then maybe they have a point."

Eddie takes both of my hands in his, kisses my

fingers—on one hand, then the other—and then leans his forehead against mine, looking me right in the eyes. "Honey. Do *you* think we're crazy?"

I stare right into his eyes, seeing him completely exposed and vulnerable in all of his emotions. "No. It feels right."

"For me too," he says. "And as long as it feels right to *us*, then to hell with everyone else."

I smirk. There's that source of confidence and determination that I've missed all of these years.

"Now what do you say we see a priest about that kid of ours?"

DECEMBER 23RD
Eddie

❄ ❄ ❄

"I remember you," Father Charlie says to Collette after she's given him a summary of our situation.

We're in one of the office spaces at Our Lady of Victory Basilica in Lackawanna. The priest offers his hands to the two chairs sitting grouped together on the other side of his desk.

"Please, let's sit," he says as he sinks into his chair. "I remember you, but vaguely. That was probably my first year ordained. What was that, 1975?"

"It was '74," Collette corrects, taking her own seat with me right beside her.

The priest nods. "Ah. Okay. That sounds about right. That *was* my first year ordained."

From what I can tell, Father Charlie is only five or six

years older than us. At our age, it's so hard to tell, though.

Collette nods. "I was still in high school back then. Oh, how long ago that was!"

"We were hoping you'd be able to help us track down the baby that she gave up," I say, trying to push the conversation in the right direction.

"Well, the child would certainly not be a *baby* anymore," Father Charlie says.

"She," Collette says. "I had a girl. Eddie and I have been calling her Lily, although I have no idea what her real name is. I don't really know anything about her."

The priest nods again. "Well, okay. It doesn't seem like we have a lot to go on, but I'll see what I can do to help. Unfortunately, the institution that helped unwed mothers back then has changed iterations over the years. Not to say that it doesn't exist anymore," he adds quickly. "We are just as committed as always to helping mothers and their children find good homes that will lead them to success in life. However, for the purposes of your search, we'll just need to track down where exactly the records regarding her adoptive placement has ended up."

"How much red tape are we looking at?" I ask. Things are quite different nowadays than they were in the 70s. "I'd imagine that there are certain privacy laws, or doesn't that pertain to you because this is a church?"

Father Charlie shakes his head. "I'm afraid I can't answer that with certainty. Before we part, I'll make sure to put you in touch with someone who can better answer that question."

Collette nods. "Okay. Thank you."

"A lot of the records from that original organization were transferred to the new one, OLV Human Services, but some were also transferred right to Erie County's Social Services department."

"Do you know which ones went where?" I'm more than a little concerned that he's still sitting here on these lounge chairs with us and not looking up anything on his computer.

Father Charlie brings his hands together and meets only his fingertips. "I can look, yes, but I do want to warn you of something first. It's two days until Christmas. A lot of the staff have taken the whole week off, with Christmas being on a Wednesday this year."

"Oh." Collette seems to shrink in on herself a bit.

"Even those who are working might be very busy. You might be better off waiting until after the first of the year."

Collette meets my eyes and I can see the panic in them without any word being said.

"No, that won't do," I say. "We're hoping to find her before Christmas."

The priest's eyebrows raise. "Well, I wish you luck in your search. You're certainly asking for a lot, but it is the season for miracles." Finally, he stands and goes to his desk, but instead of turning to his computer, he reaches for the phone. "Hi, Marla? This is Charlie. Yes, hi, I have a couple here who is looking for some help tracking down a child they gave up in the seventies. Do you have anyone over there who could help us?"

Collette takes my hand as we wait for Father Charlie to finish his phone call.

"Yes, I know that's a long time ago, but they're willing to try. You do? Okay, I'll bring them over." He hangs up the phone and turns to us. "Your miracle's working out already. There's one social worker in the office today."

"Oh, that's great news!" Collette beams.

"Sure is." Father Charlie stands and pulls on a coat, then holds the door open for us. "Follow me. It's just across the street."

"Oh, thank you!" she says as we navigate our way through the office to an exterior door.

"I haven't done anything yet," he says with a chuckle as he buttons up his coat.

"Do you think this person will be able to help us?" I have to shout so the man can hear me over the roar of the tractor trailer trucks screeching to a stop at the light on the corner.

He nods. "Sure can. And if she doesn't know, she'll be able to point you in the right direction."

"At Erie County?" I ask.

"If the record isn't across the street, then yes, the county *should* have it." He pushes the button for the crosswalk. Moments later, the light shifts and we start across the busy intersection.

"And they'll be able to look up where our daughter is?" I know I'm pushing a priest, testing the limits of someone who is only trying to help us out, but I want to make sure that we'll get the answer we want and that Collette will finally have peace with the whole thing.

"I'm not sure about that for certain, but I'm sure they could try. They'll certainly have more answers for you than I do. I'm afraid I'm not the expert in these matters."

We reach the building and Father Charlie opens the doors for us. Up on the second floor, we walk into an office that has OLV Human Services displayed on a board above the receptionist's desk.

"Father Charlie," Marla says with a smile when she sees him.

"Hello, young lady. How are you doing?"

"Just fine. I have the next three days off and I'm looking forward to spending the time with my family."

"That's great! I have to work. It's kind of the Big Guy's birthday and all," he jokes. "Anyway, I bring with me Eddie Marshall and Collette Hopkins, who are hoping to track down a baby that Collette gave up in the seventies. You said there was someone working today?"

Marla nods. "Yup. Let me just call back to Erica and see if she's free."

"Thank you, Marla." Father Charlie turns to us. "And best of luck to the both of you. I hope you find your daughter and have a very happy life together."

"Thank you!" Collette says again.

Before Father Charlie descends the stairs, he turns to Marla. "Take care of them."

"I will." She already has the phone to her ear. "Hi, Erica? Hi, that couple is here now. Father Charlie just dropped them off. Should I—oh, you'll come up for them? Okay. I'll let them know." Marla hangs up the phone and smiles warmly at us. "She'll be right out any moment. Why don't you take a seat?"

I turn and notice that there's only one seat available in the area that is designated as the waiting room. There aren't even any magazines or anything nearby to occupy someone's time while they wait. Either the wait must not be long or they don't get a lot of visitors.

We don't really have any time to contemplate taking a seat because the door to the left of the reception desk opens and another woman greets us.

"Hi! I'm Erica James. I'm one of the social workers here at OLV Human Services." She takes turns shaking each of our hands.

"I'm Eddie, and this is Collette," I say. "Thank you for agreeing to help us. I know you're one of the few working today."

"The only one, actually. Besides Marla, that is." Erica smiles at her coworker, then turns back to us and nods in the direction of the rest of the office. "Why don't you guys come on back and we can chat?"

"Thank you," Collette says and follows her through the door.

Erica leads us down a hallway and into an office on the right. I can't tell if it's small or if it just looks that way from the number of pieces of furniture crammed into the room. Two desks sit side-by-side to one another. Along the wall are several filing cabinets, with even more papers and boxes stacked on top. Tucked behind the door sits one chair meant for visitors.

Erica walks over to her neighbor's desk and pulls out the chair. "Here, one of you can sit on this too." She closes the door, then takes her seat on her chair while Collette and I settle into ours.

Once I sit, I notice that there's one huge benefit of this office: through the window, there's a beautiful view of the basilica across the street. With the fallen snow, it looks more beautiful than I've ever seen it before.

"Sorry for the small office," Erica says. "Most of our money goes into providing services for the people we help, so we have to take second-hand office furniture and we haven't been able to really upgrade the building at all. But, we're here to talk about the two of you. You're hoping to find a child you gave up for adoption?" She reaches behind her on her desk and grabs a notepad and a pen.

"Perhaps we should share our story with you first," I say. "You see, Collette and I dated back in high school when we were teenagers."

Erica flips to a clean sheet on her notepad and nods to show me she's listening.

"And then I got pregnant," Collette says. "Now, this was in—well, it was 1973 when I first became pregnant, but I gave birth in '74. My parents—both of our parents, really—were not happy about it. Not at all."

"Being that they were devout Catholics and all," I add, remembering just where it is we are.

"Not only did they want to protect us from experiencing the ridicule that would come from being teenaged parents, but they wanted us to go on and live successful lives," Collette continues.

I shake my head. "And, let's not forget the obvious reason: they were embarrassed."

Collette looks down at her hands.

"Oh, that's horrible," Erica says. "I'm sorry you had to go through that."

I hold up my finger. "Well, that's not all. They forced me and Collette to never see each other again. And shipped her off to Syracuse to have the baby quietly, then my parents gave me no other choice but to join the service."

"After our daughter was born," Collette went on, "my mother came to pick her up and brought her here to surrender the child — Lily."

Erica tries to catch Collette's eye. Her tone is soft. Gentle. Caring. "Is that what you named her?"

Collette nods, then sniffles.

Erica quickly hands her a box of tissues from her desk.

"Of course, I couldn't *actually* name her, so I know that's not her *real* name, but that's what I've been calling her for the last fifty years."

The social worker nods and gives Collette time to compose herself.

To help move the conversation along, I say, "So that's what happened. Collette and I spent our whole lives away from each other. Until two days ago when I found her on Facebook. We finally reunited yesterday and now we're getting married."

"But we need to find our daughter first," Collette says. "To tie up the last loose end that was ripped from us all those years ago."

Erica puts a hand to her chest and breathes in a deep breath. "Well. That certainly is quite the story. I'm so happy the two of you found each other after all these years. As for what I can do to help you find Lily, I'm going to need some more information from you."

"What kind of information?" Collette asks.

"Let's start with your name." Erica poises her pen over her notepad.

"Collette Hopkins."

"Have you gone by any other names?"

She shakes her head. "No. Never married, so I never changed my name." She looks over at me and smiles. "Not yet, anyway."

Erica watches our interaction and can't hold back her grin either. "Do you have any ID with you? I want to make sure I get the spelling right."

"Oh, sure! I thought you might need this." Collette pulls out her wallet from her purse and hands her license to the social worker.

After Erica records her name, she returns the ID to Collette. "Do you know the date Lily was surrendered?"

"Let's see, her birthday is May 25, 1974, so I would imagine a day or two after that." She shrugs. "Like I said, my mother is the one who surrendered her."

"And what is your mother's name? Or her name at the time of surrender?"

I can see the discomfort on Collette's face as the word *surrender* continues to come up. "Could we call it something else? 'Surrender' sounds too similar to 'abandon,' and I'm afraid it might be upsetting Collette."

Erica looks up from her notepad. "Oh. I'm so sorry! I get too caught up in the legal language sometimes. What was your mother's name at the time of Lily's birth?"

Collette smiles. "Jane Hopkins. And her maiden name is Truman, in case you need that too."

"Any information to help us track down the right case will be helpful." Erica spins in her seat until she's facing her computer. "All right, let me check some databases here."

I catch Collette's eye as Erica performs her search. She offers a sad, but hopeful smile. I give her a half-hearted grin to show her that we'll get through this together. She's not alone anymore. I know she knows what I mean because she slowly nods.

"Hmm…" Erica grumbles from her computer. "Nothing on that database."

"Father Charlie said that some of the records were transferred to Erie County," I say. "Is there a way you can check that?"

"Doing that right now," Erica says with her eyes still on the computer. "The trouble is, record keeping has changed a lot over the years. And for a long time this operated as a safe haven for mothers to bring their babies, no questions asked. That doesn't really provide any paper trail for us to follow." She taps at her keyboard, then clicks on something with her mouse. "Ah. Okay. I see."

"What did you find?" Collette asks.

"Well, Lily needed a foster home when she came to us. The 70s and 80s was around the time there was a transition from orphanages and group homes to foster homes and more one-on-one attention. Since

Lily was an infant and needed more attention than some of the older orphans at the time, that's probably why she was placed in a foster home. Nowadays, any children who is separated from their biological parents—for whatever reason—ends up in foster care. We don't have orphanages anymore. At least not in Erie County."

"Okay, so what does that tell us?" I ask.

"Well, it looks like the Infant Home contracted with Erie County to find a foster home for Lily, since her adoption was finalized through Erie County."

"Why would they do that?" Collette asks.

Erica shrugs. "I'd be guessing, but I think it's because the idea of fostering was still new and the Infant Home didn't have the number of foster parents they needed to provide care for all of their children, so they worked with the county. My guess is that they were more equipped with foster parents to care for the kids that needed them."

"So the foster parents were the ones who adopted her?" Collette asks with hope in her voice.

"I don't know. The actual record is with the county now." Erica pulls her lips tight and shakes her head. "Unfortunately, I think that office is just as empty as this one is today. I know you're anxious to find her, but you'll be better off waiting until after Christmas."

Collette's shoulders begin to shake as the sadness overcomes her. "I need to reconnect our family. I've spent my whole life alone. Every Christmas alone. I can't go through another one without knowing where my daughter is. She's a piece of me, whether I'm technically her mother anymore or not."

We've traveled all this way, only to be turned away by people taking days off. Not that I can blame them around the holidays, but it's still just as frustrating.

Erica swallows hard and I see the glistening of tears in her eyes. "I have a friend who works for Erie County Social Services. I know he's off today, but I might be able to persuade him into coming in and meeting with the two of you for a little while."

Collette smiles through her tears. "Oh, thank you!"

"You think he'll come in on his day off, right before Christmas?" I ask.

"He's Christmas shopping," Erica explains. "Which he hates. So I'm thinking he'll be looking for any excuse to cut his shopping trip short. He'll probably buy everyone on his list gift cards, then come in to work."

"Thank you!" Collette cheers, sitting up straighter in her chair.

"Well, I still need to call him," Erica warns. "He still may say no. But even if he *does* say yes, there's no guarantee that he'll be able to help you anymore than I can."

"We'll take any lead we can get," I tell her.

"Thank you for all of your help. It truly means the world to us."

She smiles. "Helping those in need. It's the nature of the season."

December 23rd
Collette

* * *

I can't help but grip the handle above the door as Eddie maneuvers his car around the tight downtown streets of Buffalo. This is about as big-city as I ever get, and I'd much rather be the passenger than the driver. Once, I was a chaperone on a field trip to New York City with my students. And while I could marvel at everything that people have created over time and how everyone can coexist together, I was just as grateful to get on the bus and come back to my quiet small town.

While Buffalo is no New York City, having to keep an eye out for parking while watching for people in the crosswalks or for traffic signals, not to mention the other cars, brings a level of anxiety to me that I'd rather not experience every day.

"Would you relax?" Eddie asks from behind the wheel. "I used to come downtown all the time when I got out of the service."

"Hasn't it only recently been cleaned up?" I ask, recalling the terrible news reports that used to come on in the eighties and nineties. "What was there down here for you to see?"

"More like, what was down here for me to *drink*," he corrects. "There has always been plenty of bars downtown. As long as you stay away from the bad parts. Nowadays, those bad parts I used to avoid are the hip parts." He turns onto a street, then groans at the line of cars on both sides. "Ah, screw it. I'll just go in the garage." He puts on his signal and shifts into a lane behind a large truck.

There's a catwalk above the street, allowing people to pass from one building to the next without going out into the cold.

"So you used to hang out downtown a lot, then?" I ask.

He shrugs. "Often enough. Then my buddies and I started going to the old man bars on Broadway, until that started to go dark too. Of course, all my friends got married and settled down and we stopped going out altogether. One buddy of mine tried to keep up a weekly poker night, but with newborns and wives, nobody could really keep the commitment except me."

"Is that around the time that you got married

too?" My eyes glance down at the class ring, now securely on my finger, and I can't help but wonder if his first wife ever wore it on hers. But then, do I really want to know that answer?

He nods. "Felt like I needed to. But my heart wasn't really into the whole idea of marriage. Not until yesterday, that is."

So many questions run through my mind about his life before me. Or rather, his life before yesterday. How long was he married for? What was his wife's name? Did he ever dream of having children with her? Who was this woman who, for a moment, claimed Eddie as her partner?

Instead of voicing all of those thoughts, I simply reach for his hand.

Just at that moment, though, the truck in front of us turns into the parking garage, with Eddie following closely behind. He doesn't even see me reach for his hand with his concentration on the road.

The car jerks forward as Eddie slams on the brakes inside the garage. The truck in front of us is waiting for another car to pull out so it can take the spot closest to the entry.

Eddie grips the steering wheel with both hands, fighting back his frustration.

My cell phone rings, and I fish in my purse to answer it. I thought I had put it on silent, but apparently not. It's a good thing it didn't ring while we were talking to Father Charlie or Erica.

"Collette? It's Maureen," she says when I answer. "What's this I hear about you getting married?"

I nod and avert my eyes from the tight confines of the parking garage. "Yes, it's true. I know it's very sudden, but it's what I've decided to do. I'll explain everything when—"

"Please don't do anything like this until we can all meet him."

"With all due respect, Maureen, I can make my own decisions." First Nancy, now Maureen. I knew my friends would be shocked, but I thought they'd offer more sympathy than this. Of course, I should've also anticipated that Nancy would tell Maureen about Eddie. I never should've told Nancy earlier when I called her.

"Of course you can, sweetie. We just want to make sure you're making the right one."

"I know what I want. And this is it. There's more to the story, and I'll fill you in on everything later, but—"

"But nothing. This is insane, Collette!"

"Again, Maureen, I can make my own choices." My eyes glance over at Eddie, who is laser-focused on the slow-moving vehicles in front of him. Still, I know he's listening in. "Eddie's a good man who loves me. He's the one I've been waiting for my whole—"

"It just seems like you're rushing into it!" Nancy calls from the background on Maureen's end of the phone. Clearly, I'm on speaker.

"Would you let me talk, Nancy?" Maureen says away from the phone.

"I would, but—"

I end the call. It's my turn to cut them off. I can't help but feel more than a little annoyed at my friends. But, they're only trying to look out for me and I can't fault them for that. I can make them wait in suspense, though. They'll learn about this in due time. Then they'll see for themselves just how good of a man Eddie is.

"More objections?" Eddie asks as he pulls into a spot.

"Just concerns," I say. "They'll get over it."

Now that the car is in park, he takes my hand and kisses it. "They'll come around. Once you're able to sit them down and explain the whole story."

I nod. "I know."

❄ ❄ ❄

INSIDE SOCIAL SERVICES is a completely different office environment than OLV Human Services. Here, we're greeted by security guards who instruct us to remove everything in our pockets and usher us through metal detectors. Warnings and public notices line the walls. The furniture in the waiting room, with all the same patterns and designs, looks stained and worn with heavy use.

I cling tighter to Eddie as we walk up to the receptionist.

"Next!" she blares, even though we're the only ones in line. In fact, there are only two other people in the waiting room. Probably a rare occurrence in an office like this that covers such a large population of people.

Eddie and I walk up. "Hi, we were just over at OLV Human Services and this woman, Erica, said that we can meet with someone here."

"Do you have an appointment?" The woman behind the glass looks bored.

"Well, no. Not really," Eddie says. "But Erica said—"

"Sir, that woman doesn't work here. She can't just make appointments for us."

"That's not—"

"Please take a seat and the next social worker available will be out to meet with you as soon as possible." Her tone sounds bored. Tired.

"Now wait a minute," Eddie starts, but I touch his arm to calm him.

"How long of a wait are we looking at?" I ask. If we have to wait, then that's what we have to do. It's disappointing, sure, but arguing with this woman is only going to aggravate both of us.

"At this rate, probably closer to forty-five minutes."

"Forty-five minutes!" Eddie blurts. "It's almost

two o'clock! Are you even going to be *open* in forty-five minutes!"

"Sir, please don't raise your voice with me."

"Eddie, calm down." It's a half-hearted attempt. I feel just as frustrated as Eddie myself, but this is going to get us nowhere.

"No, I will *not* calm down!" he blares. "We're not just waiting for the next available person. We have an appointment with someone specific. All we need to know is whether he's in yet."

"I've already told you, *sir*," she emphasizes her politeness, "that someone from another agency can't make appointments for our staff."

"Can you just tell us if he's in?" I ask, again trying to diffuse the situation.

"Who is it that you're waiting for?"

Eddie and I look at one another. Erica never mentioned any names. No one to ask for once we got here.

"Didn't the lady from OLV call ahead?" Eddie asks, his tone much quieter now.

"Not that I've heard," the woman behind the glass says. "So. You can wait for the next available person. Just like everyone else." She gestures to the chairs for extra emphasis. The look on her face tells us not to question her again.

With some effort, I manage to get Eddie over to the chairs in the waiting room. He's still fuming.

He crosses his arms. "Merry friggin' Christmas."

I pat his leg, then settle into my seat for the long wait. There's a faint odor of cigarette smoke, although it's not too strong. The other two people waiting seem to be avoiding our eyes, lest they find themselves in an argument with us—or, worse, the receptionist behind the glass.

The door back into the offices opens and a young man comes out in jeans and a hooded sweatshirt. "Is anyone here Eddie and Collette?"

I raise my hand. "That would be us."

"Perfect!" he beams. "I'm Derek. I believe you saw my friend Erica down at OLV?"

"Derek!" Eddie jumps up from his seat and shakes his hand. "It's so nice to see you. Thanks for coming in and meeting us on your day off."

"Of course, man," he says. "Anything to get me out of deciding which hand lotions to buy for my sisters. Come on back." He leads us through the door.

Before we disappear out of sight, Eddie waves to the receptionist behind the glass. She glares at him before turning back to her computer.

❄ ❄ ❄

"SO, LET ME get this straight," Derek says after we've recounted our story, and everything we learned from Erica. "You're trying to track down your *fifty-year-old* daughter?"

I nod. "Yes, that's right."

"And you didn't give birth to her here in Buffalo?"

I shake my head. "No. Out in Syracuse."

Derek rubs his chin and sits back in his chair.

"Is that a problem?" Eddie asks.

"No. No problem. It's just…unusual. In cases like this, it's usually the kid trying to track down their parents. Often times they're eighteen, or in their early twenties. Sometimes they're approaching middle age, but much later than that and most adopted kids feel secure in not knowing more information on their birth parents than what they've been told."

I nod again. "Yes, it is unusual, but I'm hoping it's not impossible."

Derek springs to life. "Let's see! What's your name?"

He asks me for all the pertinent information, just as Erica did. Only, this time, he plugs it all directly into the computer. Once he's done asking me questions, he clicks around a little and then stops and sits back and puts both hands on the top of his head.

"What is it?" Eddie asks. "Is she not in the system?"

"No, she is. I found the record."

I look over at Eddie, then try to sneak a peek of Derek's computer. "Then what's the matter?"

He sighs and closes his eyes slowly. "I'm sorry. We've hit a wall."

"What does that mean?" Eddie asks quietly.

"When the foster parents adopted her, they had a closed adoption, meaning that I cannot disclose the information of where she ended up with anyone other than the child or her adoptive parents."

"But it's been fifty years," Eddie says. "She's an adult. A grown woman. She doesn't need the protection of a closed adoption anymore."

Derek shakes his head. "It doesn't work like that. The documents are sealed. Unless she decides to inquire about the two of you, that's the only way she can gain the information. I'm sorry. There's nothing more that I can do."

I erupt into sobs. I can't help it. We've come this far, only to be turned away. And not just until after the holidays are over, but for good. There is no hope in ever seeing my daughter's face again. The only living representation of mine and Eddie's love.

"I'm sorry," I croak as I wipe at my eyes with a tissue.

Eddie pulls me into him and wraps an arm around me. It's a little awkward in the office chairs, but soothing nonetheless.

"It's just that, after years of waiting and spending the day desperately searching, our dreams of ever finding her again have been ripped away from us." I lean into Eddie, who squeezes me tighter.

"I wish there was more that I could do," Derek says quietly.

I sit up and wave his comment away. "Oh, it's not your fault. I know you're only doing your job. I just wish things were different."

"Let me walk you out," Derek says. "Did you park in the garage under the Main Place Mall? I know a shortcut that'll take you right over there without having to go outside."

"That would be nice," Eddie says. "Thank you."

Derek turns back to his desk while I try to compose myself. Eddie places his hands on my shoulders, then slides them up and down my arms.

"Are you sure you're going to be okay?" he asks.

I shrug. I'll never be okay with it. I'll always wish things had worked out differently. But there's no sense in being angry about the things in the past that cannot be changed.

"This way." Derek leads us back out into the hall and through the maze of corridors.

Eddie and I are quiet as we follow behind. My heart is heavy. It's going to take a long time for me to get through this. Luckily, I'm not completely alone anymore. I have Eddie with me now.

I take his hand and squeeze it, giving him a sad smile. Silently communicating with him that I'm glad he's here with me.

Soon we find ourselves on the catwalk I noticed from down below on the street. Derek walks us across it, then stops on the other side. He steps into a corner and waves us closer to him.

Eddie and I exchange looks, confused as to what's going on. He looks just as stumped as I am.

"All right, look," Derek says. "If it gets out that I did this, I could get fired — or worse. So I'll deny ever giving this to you, but I think it's right that you have it."

I barely register him passing the paper to Eddie. The movement is so fast.

"Just put it in your pocket and don't ask questions," Derek murmurs. "Good luck with everything," he says, louder now. More at a normal volume. "I really wish I could've helped you more."

Something about the way that he's acting tells me that he's helping us around that wall we've hit. I can't help myself and I hug him. "Thank you."

"Take care of each other," he says when we part. He offers Eddie his hand, then gives another wave before retreating back across the catwalk to the county offices.

Neither of us say anything as we make our way back to the car. The note is nowhere to be seen. Eddie has tucked it away somewhere safe.

Once we get inside the privacy of our vehicle, Eddie pulls the note from his pocket and unfolds it. His brow furrows and he sits back.

"I don't understand what I'm looking at."

I take the note from him. "What do you mean?"

Tom and Lisa Hughes.

"Does it make any sense to you?" Eddie asks.

I start to shake my head, then stop. Suddenly, I gasp as the realization hits me. "These are the names of the couple who adopted Lily!"

Eddie shrugs. "Okay. But with a name like that, they could be anywhere."

I turn and look at him, a smile across my face. "No, Eddie. I know them. They live in Batavia."

DECEMBER 23RD
Eddie

❄ ❄ ❄

The plate of cookies sitting on the table in Collette's kitchen tempts me. Collette is sitting across me, on the phone with another one of her friends from around town.

"Yes, their names are Tom and Lisa Hughes," Collette says. "I'm not sure where they live, but I need to get in touch with them."

My stomach grumbles. Since we've been gone all day, we never had a proper lunch and the large breakfast we had has worn off. Maybe just one cookie wouldn't hurt anything. It would put something in my belly until I can eat something more. No telling when we'll figure out a plan for dinner. Collette's on a roll with these phone calls.

"It's a long story," she says in the phone. "Do you remember where they—oh, I see. Okay. No, I knew it was a long shot. If you think of someone who might know where they are, give me a ring, would you? Thank you!" She hangs up the phone and sets it down on the table. Her shoulders slump. "Another one who has no idea where they are."

"We'll find them," I tell her.

"Before Christmas?"

I smirk. "Is that our deadline now?"

"Well, I don't want to spend another Christmas as a spinster. I need to know where my family is. Know they're all safe. I can't go another year without knowing. Not now that we've…"

She doesn't need to finish the thought. I'm already nodding in agreement. "I have a question."

"What's that?" She picks at a gingerbread cookie on the other side of the plate.

"How can you know the Hughes without knowing where they live or what their phone numbers are?" I ask. "When we left Buffalo, it seemed like you knew exactly who they were."

"Well, I thought Barbara would've known," she says. "She was another teacher I used to work with at the high school. Retired two years before me. But she barely remembers Lisa."

"Remembers her from where?"

"Oh, I used to work with a Lisa Hughes!" She brightens at the memory. "I remember she said her husband's name was Tom."

"Any kids? Maybe you saw Lily back then without even realizing it."

She shakes her head. "Not that I remember. But then, Lisa only worked there for about a year. She moved on to another district halfway through her second year. Since her time was short, nobody really made lasting connections with her."

"Did you have a lot of contact with her back then?"

"Not really. She taught math, I taught English. Her room was down the hall from mine. Other than faculty meetings and bumping into each other in the staff room, we didn't really have any reason to have any kind of conversation."

"What year was that? Maybe this couple isn't even the right one?"

"No. I know I'm right. I can feel it. Besides, what are the odds? And I remember that they lived in Batavia." Something seems to occur to her. "Actually, now that we're talking about it, I remember her saying something about her daughter being in first grade. Of course, I wouldn't have known her at the time, since she was in a whole different building than the one I taught in."

"Do you think Lisa Hughes knew that you were her daughter's biological mother?"

Collette breaks apart the cookie she stole from the plate. Crumbs scatter across the table. Her eyes are focused on breaking apart the cookie, not meeting mine. "Well, if what Derek at DSS said is true, then those records were sealed and would only be opened if Lily or her parents asked about it. So unless Lisa was curious, I don't think she made the connection."

"Have you considered the possibility that the Hughes have moved—"

The sound of the phone ringing interrupts my question. "Hello? Oh, hi Elaine! Thanks for calling me back. You see, I'm looking for a couple, who I think live in Batavia. I wondering if you know them."

As Collette carries on the conversation, I decide that I've had enough sugar for one sitting and get up and wander into the living room. It's dark, with the sun setting so early—the shortest day of the year was only two days ago.

I feel completely useless. I haven't lived in Batavia since I was eighteen. After the scandal that was Collette's pregnancy, even my parents moved out to the Buffalo suburbs. I had no reason to come back to Batavia. All my connections to the town I grew up in have been severed, either by physical distance, or tarnished by rumors.

The Christmas lights suddenly kick on from the timers. In an instant, the room fills with cheer from the multi-colored lights.

With Collette's voice softly carrying from the next room, and the Christmas lights shining bright, I try, for a moment, to imagine what our lives would've been like had we been together for the last fifty years. Had we not been forced apart.

I see me and Collette settling in Batavia. I see Lily making friends with the neighbors. Rushing into our bedroom to wake us up on Christmas morning. I see myself sitting on the couch with Collette as we smile and laugh while Lily opens her gifts that we had so carefully picked out, wrapped, and kept secret until the moment the surprises are revealed.

Would we have had anymore kids? Would our lives have been too hard making ends meet that we didn't have the time or the finances to have anymore kids? Or would we have waited to have more kids until we had our feet under us? By then, Lily would've probably been in school and there would be an age gap between the kids, so maybe we would've held off on having more so the kids weren't so spaced out in age.

Regardless of the number of kids we might've had, I can just picture coming home, with the house lit up with Christmas lights, smelling dinner cooking in the kitchen. Lily would run up to greet me at the door. Collette would poke her head out from the kitchen and greet me with a smile.

I've never allowed myself to dream about this before. What life would've been like with Collette. Before yesterday, this would've all been nothing but a wild, impossible dream. But now it seems like a missed opportunity. A second chance.

"Are you okay?" Collette asks in a quiet voice.

I didn't notice her enter the room. It isn't until I turn to look at her that I realize there are tears in my eyes. I sniffle and quickly wipe the tears away. "Yeah. Just thinking."

"About?" She comes up beside me and wraps her arm around me, resting her head on my chest.

"Everything. You. Lily. What things would've been like. What they still could be."

She smiles and rubs my chest, resting her head against me. "That's nice. I've been thinking a lot about that too. Over the last fifty years, whenever I had a very lonely moment, I would think about you and the love we used to have and it would always make me smile." She shifts and looks up at me. "And now we have it again and I will never let it go."

I kiss her. "Neither will I. I'm so glad we found each other again. And I'm looking forward to spending the rest of my life with you—no matter how short that might be." I grin at the joke, trying to ease the tension.

Collette slaps my chest, then nuzzles her head close against it again. "I look forward to spending many, many, *many* years with you. And those stupid jokes."

We both laugh at that.

"Any luck with the phone calls?" I ask.

She pulls away enough to look me in the eyes.

"Yes, as a matter of fact. While I was on the phone with Elaine from the library, I got a call from my friend Lynnette from church. She says that Lisa Hughes is a friend of her sister's."

I squeeze Collette's arms. Hope creeping into my heart. "Really? So she knows where she lives?"

"She's going to check with her sister, but she knows for sure she still lives in Batavia."

"Where? Does she have a phone number for her?"

Collette shakes her head. "No. Nothing like that. Like I said, she's going to check with her sister, but Lynnette is pretty sure Lisa and her husband live somewhere around the presidents street, off of South Main Street. She thought maybe Adams Street, but she wasn't sure."

"That's great!" I start toward the door, but stop when I notice how dark it's gotten. It was four-thirty last time I checked. "Oh. It's dark now."

She bypasses me and reaches for her coat on the hook by the door. "So what?"

"We're going to hunt down this couple that we've never met in the dark? Show up at their house during dinnertime and expect them to welcome us inside when we tell them we're their daughter's birth parents?"

"Well, I wasn't going to tell them that much just yet." Collette wraps her scarf around her neck. "Probably just ask where Lily is."

"But we don't even know her real name," I say. "We've been calling her Lily, but that's just what we've been calling her. How are we going to ask for her without explaining who we are? I don't want to make up a story and lie. And that's if we even find the right house. We're going to have to go door-to-door and hope that we find them."

Collette waves her hand in front of me. Her expression serious. "I don't care. We'll go door-to-door if we have to. We're going to find our daughter tonight. We've come this far. We can't give up now."

December 23rd
Collette

❄ ❄ ❄

Even I have to admit that I'm reconsidering this plan to knock on every door on Adams Street. We've tried every house along the short street, and even tried the first few on Madison Avenue, just off of Adams Street.

So far we've come up empty.

"We should head back to the car," Eddie suggests. "We've been out here an hour. Let's just warm up a bit and then we can try some more houses."

Lynette called me back half an hour ago and said that her sister couldn't remember the exact address, but was certain it was over in this area of town. Unfortunately, with the density of the houses, that doesn't really narrow it down a lot.

Slowly, I nod to Eddie and trudge back to the car in the falling snow. My hands are like ice, buried deep in my pockets and I'm not sure I'll ever feel warm again.

I can't help but feel discouraged. Twenty years ago, more people would know who their neighbors were. Maybe even be friends with them. Certainly know them by name. Nowadays, though, people barely even waved to those living next door to them. Each house, isolated from one another despite their proximity.

My own neighbors, for instance, are very friendly with me. But only the ones immediately adjacent to my house. Anyone else on the street are nearly strangers to me, despite us living so close to one another. I couldn't name them if someone were to ask. How can I expect these people to recognize the name of someone who *might* live down the street?

Eddie must pick up on my disappointment. "We'll find someone who knows them."

"Will we, though? And even if we do, how are they supposed to feel when pure strangers come literally off the street and lay claim to the daughter they've known, loved, and raised her whole life?" I shake my head. "I'm starting to feel like this is impossible."

"Don't say that. We'll come back out first thing in the morning. Since Christmas Eve is basically its own holiday, there are more people who will likely be home. Maybe we can finally catch Tom and Lisa, or someone who knows where they live." He wants to reach out to me. To console me. I can *feel* it. But the weather leaves both of us huddled into our jackets.

I shake my head. "What if they went on vacation? What if they've already left and taken Lily with them?"

"Have hope. After all, we found each other, against all odds. We'll find Lily too. And, truthfully, in the end it won't matter whether we find her on Christmas Day or some random Tuesday. It'll be a memorable day regardless."

I sigh. "Yeah."

I know he's right. I know that the day we reunite with Lily will be one that I cherish for the rest of my life. But I can't help but feel like the clock is ticking and we need to find her sooner than later. It feels like we've already wasted so much time already. I don't want to waste anymore. Not when she's right under our nose.

We reach the car, where Eddie parked it on Adams Street in front of a small blue ranch with a red front door. As we're about to get in, the door to the ranch opens and a woman pokes her head out.

"Do you two need help with something?" she calls.

"Perks of being old," Eddie jokes. "People are always trying to be helpful."

"Shush," I tell him, then turn to the woman. "We're trying to find someone who lives around here, but we're not sure who."

"I've lived on this street for years! Maybe I can help. Who is it you're looking for?"

"Tom and Lisa Hughes," I call back snow-covered across the yard. An illuminated Rudolph sits beside a Nativity scene. "I used to work with Lisa a while ago and I don't remember where exactly she lives." God forgive me for the white lie.

"Oh, well, Tom died earlier this year. Heart attack. Very sudden. But Lisa still lives in the same house they've always lived in." She points down the street. "Down on Roosevelt Avenue, right across from Adams."

"That's right!" I say, playing along with the fib. "Thank you!"

"But you won't catch Lisa. As far as I know, she's at work."

Eddie and I exchange confused looks. What would a teacher be doing working after six o'clock on December 23rd?

"But…it's after school hours," I say.

"School? Lisa doesn't work for a school. Not in years! No, she's a nurse. She works for the VA. More money in nursing than teaching."

The Veteran's Affairs hospital. Across town.

I nod slowly. My own fears about my pension lasting with the rising cost of living comes to the surface. "Okay. Thank you! I'll have to try some other time, then!"

"No problem! I'll tell her you were looking for her. What's your name?"

"Collette," I say without even thinking. I just hope that we find Lisa before the neighbor does.

"I'm Janice. If you need anything, you know where to find me! Merry Christmas!"

"Merry Christmas!" Eddie calls with a wave. "And thank you!"

We hurry inside the car, where Eddie turns it on and then blasts the heat.

Even though it's blowing out cold air, we both run our frozen hands over the vents.

"So what now?" Eddie asks. "Do you want to come back tomorrow?"

I look at him with my eyebrows scrunched together. "Tomorrow? No. We're going to the VA. We know where Lisa is now."

"And how exactly do you suggest we find her?"

"Ask for her by name if we have to," I say. "We're so close, Eddie! I'm not letting Lily slip through our fingers any longer."

Eddie smiles. "You know, your maternal side has really come out today. It looks good on you."

I return the smile. "Thanks."

He shifts into gear and drives off.

DECEMBER 23RD
Eddie

❄ ❄ ❄

The VA Hospital sits stately at the end of a long yard, which is now blanketed with snow. We find a parking spot along the entry road, among all the other cars coming and going. It's busier than I thought it would be for a Monday night. Then again, I haven't thought much about this place since I moved away from Batavia fifty years ago.

Collette and I rush to get to the main doors. The wind has started to pick up, throwing flakes in our faces and making me reminiscent of the song that had just been playing on the radio, cheerfully recalling Jack Frost nipping at your nose.

I hold the door open for Collette, who hurries inside. Her eyes dart around once we're out of the cold, trying to get our bearings.

It's busy, with people coming and going in all directions. Many of them are carrying food, some are toting chairs, while others seem to be directing the flow of traffic.

I pull Collette to the side so we're not in the way.

"We're so close," she says with a smile on her face. She lifts up onto her toes to try to see into the crowd. "Something is about to happen. I can *feel* it."

So can I, but I want to tread carefully. I don't want either of us to be completely heartbroken if things don't turn out the way we hope. "Collette, just be careful—"

We stand aside as a group of carolers come in, each of them clutching their sheet music.

"Any idea which one is Lisa?" Collette asks.

Figuring this isn't the time or the place to talk about adjusting our expectations, I say, "Well, Lisa would be at least our age. Probably older, actually. But, Collette—"

She shakes her head. "I can't see anyone our age. Everyone looks so young. What if she's not here? What if Janice was wrong? What if we'll never find her? What if we never meet Lily?" Her voice grows louder and louder as panic sets in.

I put my hands on her shoulders and look around the room myself. "Shh…we'll find her. We just need to have a clear head." I notice one young woman directing people by the door. "Stay here."

As I approach, the person the young woman was talking to walks away. "Hi, are you a volunteer, or are you here to visit someone?"

I shrug. "Well…more the latter. I was wondering if you know of a nurse named Lisa who works here. We're trying to—"

The woman apparently doesn't care to hear my reasoning. She points across the room. "If she's a nurse, she'll be in the dining room helping some of our volunteers set up for the annual Christmas Eve feast tomorrow night. Not only will we have the residents here, but all the veterans from the area are invited, and, of course, local politicians."

I raise my eyebrows. *Of course* local politicians. Which one of them would pass up a photo opportunity?

"Look for someone in scrubs," she adds.

"You said she'll probably be in the dining room?" I ask.

The woman nods and waves me away as she turns to another person.

I look back for Collette, but can't find her in the spot beside the door where I had left her. My eyes scan the busy room, panic starting to come over me, but then I hear her voice right in front of me.

"What did you find out?"

She doesn't notice how much I jump, which I'm grateful for. "Probably in the dining room. Look for someone in scrubs."

"Oh. Good point."

We squeeze our way through the doorway and into the stately dining room, which has been beautifully adorned for Christmas. Lighted garland lines the walls. A large Christmas tree sits in front of the window. It has to be at least ten feet tall, if not taller. Red bows add more color to the decorations, as well as the battery-powered tea lights along the rows of tables. A wreath hangs above the ornate fireplace, complementing the beautiful architecture of the building.

"There are several people in scrubs," Collette says.

"So let's just ask someone," I say. "We haven't come this far without a little help." I find the closest nurse. A man in powder blue scrubs. "Is there a nurse by the name of Lisa here? Lisa Hughes?"

He nods. "Over there. She's helping some of the residents set up for the feast tomorrow."

"Thank you." I lead Collette across the room, where I spot an older woman in the same powder blue scrubs as the man I had just asked. Lisa Hughes is older, for sure, but she looks young. Thin, still with a lot of color in her hair, and a smile that seems to brighten the room.

I only hope that our Lily picked up the same kindness that seems to radiate from Lisa.

Collette clings to my arm as we approach her.

Lisa is setting out place settings with a man in a

wheelchair. She smiles when she sees us approach. "Hello! Are you here to help or here to visit?"

Collette shakes her head. "No, we're neither."

"Um…" I look around the crowded room. "Is there someplace private that we can talk?"

Lisa seems taken aback by the request, but smiles nonetheless. "Sure." She turns to the man in the wheelchair. "Jim, just keep setting those place settings. I'll be right back."

She stands and leads us through a different door at the back of the dining room. It seems to be a hallway for loading food for the daily meals. It's not entirely private, but it's quieter here than in the noisy dining room.

"I'm sorry, but do I know you two?" she asks.

"Um…not exactly." I rack my brain for how to go about this. I guess a part of me never thought that we'd get to this point today. Two days ago, I thought I'd be spending the holidays alone, and now, not only have I rekindled a love I thought had died, but I'm about to be reunited with the child that I never met and has changed the trajectory of my life.

Collette takes a breath. "My name is Collette, and this is Eddie. You and I actually used to work together, back when you were teaching."

"Oh yeah?" The way she says it indicates that she doesn't remember. "Gosh, that was a whole other lifetime! It's good to see you!"

"You too." Collette offers a polite smile, then

presses on with her story. "When Eddie and I were teenagers, I became pregnant—"

Lisa's face turns. She starts to shake her head and back away from us. Her face has melted into shock, bordering on fear. "No. No! Ella is *my* daughter. Not yours!"

"Ella," Collette says under her breath.

The name hits me too. The daughter we've been calling Lily is really named Ella. Ella Hughes.

"You gave her up!" Lisa cries.

"Lisa, please," Collette says. "We're not trying to replace you and your late husband as Ella's parents. We just want to get to know her."

Lisa steps to the door, but before she leaves, she turns to us. "You know, this is the first Christmas since I've lost my husband. Don't take away my daughter too."

"But we're not trying to—" Collette puts a hand on my arm to stop me from protesting any further.

Lisa disappears into the noisy dining room again, leaving Collette and I alone. Brokenhearted.

"Well," I say, "we tried."

Collette leans into me and starts crying. Not as much as she has throughout the day, but tears of sadness nonetheless. Fate is truly out of our hands now. We can only hope that Lisa changes her mind and decides to tell Ella that we came asking about her.

Of course, other than our first names, Ella would

have less information than we do to find us. Not unless she knows to check with Erie County Social Services to find us.

I hold Collette tightly against me. Tears prickle my eyes, but I clear my throat from any emotion. "We'll find her. Eventually. Might not be today, or tomorrow, or even six months from now, but someday we'll see her again."

"Ella," Collette says. "It's a beautiful name."

"I wonder what her middle name is."

She pulls away enough to look at me. "I wonder what she looks like."

"She'll probably have the dark hair you used to have."

"And I'm sure she'll have your eyes."

"Even if she doesn't, she'll be perfect."

She leans back into me. "But not ours."

I rest my chin on the top of her head. "No. Not really." I take a breath. "But that doesn't mean we can't get to know who she is. Maybe. If she'll let us."

"If her *mother* will let us."

Now I pull away and give her an eye. "If you found out that your mother didn't want you to do something, what is the first thing that you would do?"

She smirks. "Try to find a way around it. I avoided breaking things off with you when my mother demanded it, all those years ago. We snuck around for two weeks before my mother put me in a car and dropped me off at my aunt's house." She sighs. "Those were some dark times. It took me forever to forgive my mother."

"And now we're correcting those mistakes," I say.

"I regret giving her up. So much. So what if we weren't married? So what if we were young? We would've figured it out. I wish we could've been a family."

"I do too. But I know that things worked out the way they were supposed to."

Collette jerks away from me. She turns her back to me and crosses her arms. "Oh, is this the 'everything happens for a reason' speech? That's not what I need to hear right now."

"I think it is," I push. "Think about your dedication to your students over the years. All the groups you volunteer for. You were able to give your time to all of those people who needed you because your focus wasn't split on a family. You could give more to everyone than others who had families because that was where you found joy. Fulfillment."

She sighs, and I know she's listening.

"And me. I went into the service. That was always the plan. And it still would've been, even if I had you and Ella to come home to. Because we would've needed the money. It would've been so hard for us back then."

"But we would've figured it out," she snaps. "Instead, we weren't even given the chance."

"And if we had been given the chance, faced against all of those challenges, what would that have done to our relationship? We wouldn't have had the reunion we had yesterday. And what miracles our love has performed since then!" I step closer to her, putting a hand on her shoulder. "Collette, I've been divorced. I know how that feels. And, trust me, the only thing that would hurt more than having to wait fifty years to be reunited with you is to watch our marriage crumble because we let life get in the way. Get the better of us. And there's a good chance that's what being teenaged parents would've done to us."

Collette's shoulders sag as she gives in to my line of reasoning. "You're probably right. But this doesn't seem fair. Ella's a grown woman! She probably has kids of her own. Shouldn't she get to decide whether she wants to get to know us, and not her mother?"

I hug her tight, again resting my chin on her head. "I know. But when is life fair? All we can do is embrace the good moments and make the best of it."

She looks up and kisses me. "I love you. And I can't wait to be your wife. Finally."

I smile. "I love you too. Hey, why don't we salvage what's left of today and retire back at your place? I think it's about time that I finally get into the spirit of the season."

She offers a sad smile. "I'd like that."

DECEMBER 23RD
Collette

❄ ❄ ❄

*I*cling to Eddie's hand as we maneuver through the crowd filling the dining room, then through the lobby of the VA toward the exit. It reminds me of a busy bee hive's nest, the way everyone moves about with their own set of obligations to work toward a common goal.

At the door, Eddie steps out just as a middle-aged woman and a boy come up the steps, each carrying a large box in their hands. I stand back inside while Eddie holds the door open for them out in the cold.

We smile politely at each other as the woman offers a quick, "Thank you" to Eddie as she passes by. Based on my years teaching, I'm willing to bet that the boy with her is probably around twelve or thirteen. Not quite high school age yet, but close enough.

"Do you need help with that?" I offer.

"No, thank you," the woman says. "We've got it." Turning to her son, she says, "Do you see Grandma anywhere?"

My head turns and my eyes follow the mother and son as they walk into the busy lobby. Something in my heart tells me to be still.

"Collette? What's the matter?" Eddie asks from behind me.

"Shh!" I hiss, keeping my eyes locked on the mother and son.

The woman is definitely middle-aged. The wrinkles that showed around her eyes when she smiled and said thank you at the door were proof enough. But there's more to it than that. There's a certain way that she dresses—in a black pea coat with a belt tied at her waist. Jeans. Khaki boots. The way that she carries herself, as if she's had some life experience that has given her a sense of confidence, but also generosity and kindness.

Somehow, I know that there's a connection between us. There's something about the woman who reminds me of…me. About fifteen years ago. Or more precisely, *seventeen* years ago.

The next instant confirms it. Lisa holds her arms out and hugs the woman and the boy. The woman and Lisa move into easy conversation, both of them in relaxed postures, as if they have a relationship that has seen it all. One that doesn't require formal introductions.

Like mother and daughter.

Tears spill from my eyes. I've shed more tears today than I have all year, but these are finally happy tears.

I've found her.

"Collette, honey, what's wrong? Why are you crying?" Eddie asks beside me.

Now that I know who she is, I can't take my eyes off of her. Instead, I point. "Eddie, that's her. That's Lily—or rather, Ella. That's our daughter."

"Where?" he asks.

"Right there! Talking to Lisa! The one who just walked past us."

"Oh." Eddie's eyes widen in surprise as he finally locates her. "She's beautiful. Just like you."

Instinct kicks in and I rush toward her. Toward them all. I don't think about what I'll say or what I'll do, or even the fact that Lisa told us to leave and to not bother any of them. I have to talk to Ella. I have to tell her who I am. Who we are.

I barely register Eddie calling my name behind me. I ignore him anyway.

"Hi," I blurt once I'm standing next to Lisa, Ella, and the boy.

Ella looks at me, confused, but polite. "Oh, hello."

Lisa shoots daggers at me. "Excuse me, I thought I—"

"My name is Collette." I can't take my eyes off of

Ella. Eddie's right. She is beautiful. And she has the dark hair I used to have before mine started to turn gray, and she certainly has Eddie's eyes. Exactly the way that we predicted.

"I thought I told you to get out of here!" Lisa shouts. "I need someone's help here! Security!"

Eddie is beside me, his hand on my elbow. "Collette, we shouldn't—"

Ella's eyes look up at him and the connection sparks between the two of them.

"Honey, I'll be right back," Lisa says. "You shouldn't have to deal with—"

"Wait, Mom," she says, her eyes still focused on Eddie. Finally, she pulls her gaze away long enough to meet her mother's eyes. "Why don't you take Donnie somewhere and put him to work? I'll meet up with you guys when I'm done here."

Lisa grabs her daughter's arm. "Ella, please."

Ella smiles at her and pats her arm. "It's okay, Mom. Really."

With reluctance, Lisa pulls at her grandson, leading him away. Before they go, she shoots a nasty look at Eddie and me. But beyond that look, I can see that what's she's really feeling is hurt. And fear.

When Lisa and Donnie are gone, Ella smiles at us. "Sorry about that. My mom can be…heated, sometimes."

"It's okay. I understand." I nod, tears filling my eyes again.

"You said your name is Collette?" she asks.

"That's right. And this is Eddie. We're…well, I'm the woman who…um…the woman who gave birth to you."

I make sure I'm careful not to call myself her mother. I haven't parented this woman. I haven't gotten up with her in the middle of the night for feedings. I haven't cheered on her softball games or cried when she went off to prom. I haven't shaped her to be the woman that she is today. But I *am* a part of her life. Her reason for life.

"And I helped," Eddie jokes from beside me.

Ella's eyebrows shoot up. "Oh! So you're my…parents?"

I shake my head. "No. Lisa is your mother. And Tom was your father. We're just the ones who…created you, I suppose. And, if you're willing, we'd like to get to know you. Finally."

She touches her forehead. "Wow. Okay. This is a lot to take in. I, uh, I've always known that I was adopted. My parents weren't shy about that. But they never really entertained my questions about my birth parents—about you guys. And since my parents—Tom and Lisa—since they were so wonderful to me, I've never felt the need to really pursue it beyond just wondering." She takes a breath. "I think I need to sit down."

Eddie rushes to find the nearest seat. Of course, there isn't one, so we settle on a built-in bench along the outer wall of the lobby. Eddie and I take the spots on either side of her.

"So, tell me, what made you decide to give me up for adoption?" she asks after she's had a minute to catch her breath.

For the final time today, we recount our story. How we fell in love as teenagers in the early seventies. How I became pregnant. How different things were back then, so our parents were quite upset about the idea. I tell her about having to stay with an aunt for the duration of my pregnancy. How I gave birth to her in Syracuse, then my mother brought her back to Buffalo to drop her off at the Infant Home. How Eddie and I were forced apart until we found each other only yesterday.

"Oh wow," she says once we've finished. "That seems like—you just never really know what someone's going through—even when it's your own story."

"I can't stress enough that we don't want to replace your parents," I say. "I know your mom is obviously very upset, but we want to get to know her too."

Ella smiles and nods. "She'll be happy to hear that. And she'll come around. This is her first Christmas without my dad, and it's been rough on her. She went back to work so she doesn't have to sit at home without him. She throws herself into every project she can to avoid feeling lonely. And now when you guys show up, I think she's afraid she's going to lose me too."

"She'll never lose you," Eddie says.

"I know. And she'll get that too. Eventually. It's just a lot to process."

"Sorry," I say. "I can't imagine what it's like from your perspective."

"It's a lot," she admits. "But it's good, you know?" She looks between the two of us and reaches for our hands. "I've always wondered what you were like. Whenever we'd have family pictures, I could tell that I didn't quite look like my parents. They're all blonde and I have dark hair—and it's starting to get more gray than I would like."

"That won't change," I joke, indicating my own hair. "Not unless you dye it."

She waves that off. "Who has time for that? No, I'm happy with the way I look. I'm happy with my life. I've had a good life. Um…what else? Let's see…I'm married. For twenty-five years now, if you can believe it! We have three kids." She nods toward the dining room. "I brought my youngest with me because I just picked him up at a birthday party at the ice skating rink." She smiles and shrugs, squeezing our hands. "I don't really know where to go from here. It's hard for me to catch you up on the last fifty years of my life. But I'm looking forward to sharing it all with you. And getting to know you both."

"So are we, honey," I tell her.

"You can feel however you want for us, but just know that we love you," Eddie adds.

"We always have," I say.

Ella smiles. "You know, it's strange. Throughout my life, I almost think that I could feel that love. Even from afar. Even though this is our first time officially meeting."

"Good. I'm so glad." I move some of her hair out of her face. "And I'm so happy that you've been happy. That makes the decision I made all those years ago a little easier to remember."

Ella looks over to the dining room. "Well, I suppose I should go help my mom. Or rather, relieve Donnie from the labor she's subjecting him to."

I laugh and stand, along with Ella and Eddie. "We'd love to meet your husband and children too. When you're ready."

Ella looks between us. None of us really knowing how to say goodbye. We've spent all day tracking her down and now that we've found her, it seems silly to just go home as if nothing's changed. But Ella has her own life that she needs to get back to. And Eddie and I have a wedding to plan.

"Can I hug you?" she asks.

"Of course!" I say. "I was hoping you would ask!"

The three of us wrap each other in a hug. A family, long separated, finally reunited.

"I'm so glad you found me," she says into our ears.

And just like that, all the frustration and aggravation and worry that I've felt today is suddenly all worth it.

CHRISTMAS EVE
Eddie

❄ ❄ ❄

"Go in peace," the priest says at the end of Mass. "And Merry Christmas!"

Immediately, the organ kicks in and one of the singers in the balcony bursts out into a happy rendition of "Joy to the World." The congregation joins in singing the first verse, but as the singer above us moves into the second verse, the crowd starts to disperse.

Parents with young children help them into their jackets before sneaking down the side aisle toward the door. The elderly begin getting situated in their coats, reaching for their canes, and smiling at each other before shuffling down the main aisle.

As the song comes to a close, the murmur of voices begins to rise as idle chatter erupts. Some people stand around and wish each other merry Christmas. Others hurry out the door, anxious to continue their holiday celebrations.

Two women rush up to Collette with bright eyes and smiles.

"Collette! Is this him?" one of them asks.

She smiles. "Yes. This is Eddie. Eddie, this is Maureen and Nancy." She hooks her arm in mine and leans her head against my shoulder.

I shake each of their hands. "It's nice to meet you both. Collette says that you're two of her best friends."

"Yes, we've known Collette for a long time," Nancy says.

"And we're very protective of her, so don't do anything to hurt her!" Maureen pokes me in the chest.

"I plan on being the best husband for her," I say. "I've waited long enough to call myself her husband. I'm not going to mess it up." I look down at Collette and she smiles. I want to kiss her so badly, but decide to hold off while we're in the company of her friends. And God. We've already made out once in church, let's not add another indiscretion.

"Aw," Nancy coos as she places a hand on her chest. "That's so sweet. Ugh, you two make me miss my late husband. We had such a happy marriage."

Maureen exchanges a look with Nancy, then turns back to us. "We'd love for you both to come to

Christmas dinner tomorrow. At either of our houses. We want to get to know you, Eddie, and what better time to do it than when we're celebrating with friends and family? Nancy was planning on coming over to my house after her daughters both go home with the kids."

Collette and I look at each other and smile.

"No, that's okay," Collette says. "But thank you for the invite. We already have plans."

"You do?" Nancy asks. "What are your plans? I thought you said you wanted to spend Christmas alone?"

She shrugs. "Some things have changed. A lot of things, actually."

"So then what are your plans for tomorrow?" Maureen asks.

Collette smiles at me again before answering. "We're going to our daughter's house for Christmas."

It's funny to watch both women's eyes burst open in surprise.

"Your daughter?" Nancy gasps.

"Since when do you have a daughter?" Maureen adds.

"It's a long story," Collette says with a smirk.

Up on the altar, I see the priest come out of the sacristy and nod to me. I tug on Collette's arm. "I think we're up."

Collette follows my line of sight. "Oh! Yes, we are. We have to go."

"Go?" Maureen turns her head up to the altar. "Go where?"

"What's going on?" Nancy asks.

As we start to shuffle out into the aisle ourselves, Collette says, "I'm sorry, but I'll have to explain it later. We need to go."

Nancy nods, a thought occurring to her. "Yes, I put my oven timer on too. I should probably get back to it. I'm always afraid that it's going to burn the house down."

Collette laughs and waves it off. "Oh, no! Not the oven. We're getting married tonight."

Nancy and Maureen's faces drop in shock.

"Honey, we should probably go," I nudge.

"Wait!" Maureen calls as we start up the center aisle.

"You're getting married *tonight*? But you had no plans to get married two days ago!" Nancy says as she follows behind us too.

Finally, Collette turns back to them. "I told you, I'll explain everything later. For now, though, will you girls be our witnesses?"

Nancy and Maureen exchange glances again. Both of them seem unsure. But I can tell that they're slowly accepting the fact that they're powerless to stop what's about to happen.

"Yes, of course we will," Nancy says.

"Are we ready?" Father Thomas asks once we're at the altar.

Collette looks at me again. "Finally, I think we are."

"I've waited fifty years for this day," I tell her. "I don't want to wait any longer."

One Year Later
Collette

* * *

"Merry Christmas!" I cheer as I set the basket of baked goods on the counter behind the circulation desk at the library.

Elaine and Lynette jump out of their seats.

"Oh, more treats!" Elaine says. "What have you got for us?"

"Cinnamon swirl muffins, gingerbread cookies, and some sourdough bread." I point out each thing in the red basket. "I tried to keep a wide palette."

"It's all bread and it'll all stick to my hips," Lynette says. "But I'm going to eat it anyway."

"It's Christmas, let yourself live a little!" Elaine bites into a gingerbread.

"Are you girls only here a half day?" I ask.

They nod. In years past, I would've volunteered on Christmas Eve just so I wasn't alone. And it would help pass the time for the girls at the library. But last year I broke that tradition, and I don't think I'll be returning to it. Eddie and I have plans today. Plans that I'm very excited about.

"You didn't have to stop in here today," Lynette says as she picks at the top of the muffin. "It's your first anniversary."

I wave it off. "Oh, I know. And I won't stay long, but I would've missed seeing you girls. I just wanted to bring a little holiday cheer to one of the slowest days in the library this year."

"Well, we appreciate it," Elaine says as she finishes her cookie.

"What are you and Eddie up to today?" Lynette asks.

I smile. "It's hard to believe it's been a year. I feel like a teenager again. Still feels like we're on our honeymoon."

That honeymoon, of course, didn't happen until this past summer. Two weeks traveling around Europe, seeing things I had resigned myself to never get to see in my life. All beside a man I thought I'd never see again. It was wonderful.

Not only did we have no travel plans after our wedding last Christmas Eve, but neither of us could stand the idea of leaving our daughter just after we had found her. We spent six months figuring out how we could operate in each other's lives. We got to know each other, warmed up to Ella's family, and shared more stories about our lives from the last fifty years. It wasn't until after all of that that Eddie and I both felt comfortable enough with our relationship with our daughter to go on a long trip.

"We're just going to spend the day together," I say. "Eddie would've come with me this morning, but he said he wanted to get the driveway shoveled before it snows again tonight. Says it keeps him young."

"Well, with these cookies at home, he's going to need the exercise," Elaine jokes. "These are delicious!"

"You enjoy them." I start toward the opening in the counter, right by the door. "You girls have a Merry Christmas! I'll see you in the New Year!"

"You too, Collette!" Lynette calls.

"Thank you, again!" Elaine adds.

THE DRIVEWAY IS clear when I pull into it only ten minutes later. Eddie and our neighbor Kyle are still standing on the sidewalk, both of them leaning on their shovels. They wave as I pull in and put the car in park.

"You're still out here?" I ask Eddie when I come around the back of the car.

"You've only been gone for twenty minutes!" he says, then leans over and greets me with a kiss.

I make sure that only my lips touch his. Shoveling is a workout for him, and the sweat that he produces from it sure shows its effects. "You're going to need to take a shower before we go."

"I was planning on it."

"How've you been, Kyle?" I ask. "Merry Christmas. Make sure to tell Janelle that as well."

He nods and smiles. "Merry Christmas to you too. We're doing well. In fact, I came out here to shovel the driveway, but your husband beat me to it."

Husband. That title still brings a smile to my face.

"Well, he's been known to manage the neighborhood," I say.

After we got married, Eddie sold his house in Cheektowaga and moved in with me. It was a bit of an adjustment, having lived in the house by myself for so long, but one we were both willing to make. The sale of his house even helped pay for our honeymoon.

Since then, Eddie has been making a name for himself in my neighborhood. Greeting the neighbors. Helping them mow their lawns, fix squeaky porch steps, tinkering with their cars. He even has a list of people who routinely ask him to change their oil. I keep telling him that he should charge a small fee for it, but Eddie says that he just likes being the friendly handyman of Union Street.

"I appreciate it," Kyle says. "You've saved me a lot of time."

Eddie waves it off. "Meh. I don't mind. Keeps me young! Everyone else my age seems to have moved south for the winter. Not me. I never want to lose my tolerance for the cold. I've been in much worse conditions than this!"

I roll my eyes with a smirk. Here he goes again, about to tell stories from when he was in the service.

"We should head in, dear," I tell him before he can get started. "You need to take a shower and I want to get started on that dish we're bringing later." I wave to our neighbor. "It was nice seeing you again, Kyle! Merry Christmas!"

"Merry Christmas!" he calls.

❄ ❄ ❄

LATER, WE MAKE our way across town to Meadowcrest Drive. When Eddie pulls in the driveway, I feel my heart race a little. We've spent so much time here, but this is a little different. This is the first major holiday when we're seeing Ella. Almost the anniversary of the first time we met. It feels monumental. Significant.

I hold my pot of stuffing in my hands as Eddie grips my elbow and helps me to the door. We ring the bell and wait for it to open.

Not even ten seconds later, our Ella stands in the

threshold. Just as beautiful as always.

She smiles warmly at us. "Hello! Come on in! The gang's all here and we're ready to eat!"

We step into the warm, inviting house. The murmurs of happy chatter carry from the dining room, where Ella's husband and three children sit.

"Take a seat," Scott, Ella's husband, tells us.

Ella takes the pot of stuffing from my hands so we can sidle into seats beside her three boys. An assortment of cookies sits in the middle of the table, although it doesn't seem as though anyone has touched any of them yet.

Ella disappears into the kitchen.

"How've you been?" Scott asks.

I nod. "Good. Been busy at work?" Scott runs a landscaping company. In the summer he mows lawns mostly. In the winter he plows driveways.

"It's been a good year for business," he says. "I've also contracted with a few of the cemeteries too, to keep those clear in the winter. I'm hoping to be able to work with a few businesses in town, but we'll see. For now, I think I'm at capacity."

"If you're ever in a bind and looking for a driver, give me a ring," Eddie says.

"You have your CDL?"

"Well, no. But how hard could it be? I've driven big machinery before."

I laugh. My husband, the helper. No matter how big the job.

"All right, here we go," Ella calls just before bringing out the turkey on a large platter.

Followed behind her with another dish in her hands is Lisa. She greets us with a tight smile. "Eddie. Collette. Merry Christmas."

I return the smile. "Merry Christmas, Lisa. Thanks for having us."

"Of course. You're family."

My heart bursts. Over the last year, Lisa has taken a long time to adjust to our presence in her daughter's lives. We've tried our best to be respectful of it, taking small victories along the way. Calling us family seems like a major win and I fight like crazy not to let my emotion get the better of me at Christmas Eve dinner.

The room is quiet as everyone watches our exchange, sensing the emotion pulsating in the room.

"Well," I croak, then clear my voice. "Let's eat!"

Behind the Book
A Christmas Family

❄ ❄ ❄

Adoption is something that is very important to me. My family would not exist without adoption. So with this book, I wanted to tell the story from a different perspective—that of the parents who willingly gave up the child. I can only imagine the pain and sacrifice that takes in order to come to that decision. There is an instinctive response that kicks in when we become parents—biologically or not—and to have that feeling, even if only temporarily, and then give up the child because you know it'll have a better life with a different set of parents seems like the biggest testament of bravery and faith that everything will work out for the best.

The idea for this book first came to me during the

Christmas season of 2019. At the time, I was back in grad school, doing full-time coursework after working a full-time job. It was the end of the semester, I was working on final projects and I just needed a break. I would try to convince myself that listening to instrumental Christmas music while I worked would help me focus, but what it ended up doing was allowing me permission to keep YouTube open, which kicked off an endless clicking of videos.

At some point, I landed on this video of an elderly couple, who, after years of being forced apart because of a teenaged pregnancy, finally found each other and had gotten married shortly after reconnecting.

Now, I'm not going to pretend to remember the details of that video. By the time I sat down to plot out this book in November 2023, I made an attempt to find that video from four years earlier, but I couldn't find it. Luckily, when I was procrastinating those final projects, I had finally felt inspired to jot down some ideas (a lot of ideas) about what I wanted this book to be like. I knew it would be a special one. An easy one to write. And so when it finally came time to work on it, everything flowed naturally.

That's saying something, considering the fact that my life was completely different from the time I first saw that video and got inspired to write this story. During the first draft, I was writing this book on my breaks at work, in the mornings before work, after work beside my son while he watched the same episodes of Mickey Mouse Clubhouse over and over again. A family created because of adoption.

I hope this story brings out that sense of hope that first inspired me to write it. When you're done reading, please leave a review online to help other readers decide whether the book is a good fit for them too. Thanks for reading!

Acknowledgments

This project would not have been possible without the support of my Kickstarter backers! Thank you all for your support!

Heiko Koenig
Anonymous Reader
Barbara Weintz
John Idlor
Marguerite G
Anonymous
Eron Wyngarde
Mary P. McCray
Gary Phillips

Julie Griffiths has had a crush on one of her friends at her hometown bar forever, but he's oblivious to her feelings. So when he and the rest of Julie's friends dare her to sneak into the Thanksgiving Day Parade in New York City, she accepts in order to impress her crush. Hours later, she finds herself on a crowded bus, equipped with nothing more than determination.

Brian Moore was already planning on going home to New York City for Thanksgiving, but a sudden breakup with his girlfriend gives him another reason. Heartbroken and lost, Brian isn't too happy when a woman sits beside him on the bus ride back to the city. Especially when she starts talking about her crazy idea to get into the Thanksgiving Day Parade.

Wanting to avoid an awkward encounter with his family, Brian agrees to help Julie accomplish her goal after it becomes painfully obvious that she has no plan for achieving it. But as the two begin to spend more time together, Julie starts to question her feelings for her friends back home while Brian realizes that maybe Julie is who he has been waiting for all along.

A chance moment. A snow storm. And the gift of a new beginning.

Tristan is ready to party and ring in the New Year by kissing his soon-to-be girlfriend, Julie. The only bad note in his rocking night is the ongoing snow storm. Outside his apartment, he's almost hit by a swerving car! Behind the wheel is Grace, the most beautiful woman with haunting green eyes. She's on her own mission to get home to her grandfather.

In a selfless act reminiscent of the age of knights and chivalry, Tristan vows to get her home…never realizing they are both on a date with destiny and their lives will be forever changed by the SNOW AFTER CHRISTMAS…

MORE BY THE AUTHOR

To find more books by the author, visit
DavidNethBooks.com/Books

* * *

Subscribe to his newsletter to be the first to know of new
releases and special deals!
DavidNethBooks.com/Newsletter

* * *

If you enjoyed the book, please consider leaving a review
on Goodreads or the retailer you bought it from. Reviews
help potential readers determine whether they'll enjoy a
book, so any comments on what you thought of the story
would be very helpful!

About the Author

D. Allen is the author of the sweet small town romance series, Montana Beach and Small Town Christmas.

Also writes fantasy and superhero fiction as David Neth.

www.DavidNethBooks.com
www.facebook.com/DavidNethBooks